IT CALLS ME

AN ANTHOLOGY

KATIE COUGHRAN

MONSTER IVY PUBLISHING

Cover design by Cammie Larsen

Cover image from Shutterstock.com

Interior images from pixabay.com

Hanging Tree photograph by Josiah Coughran

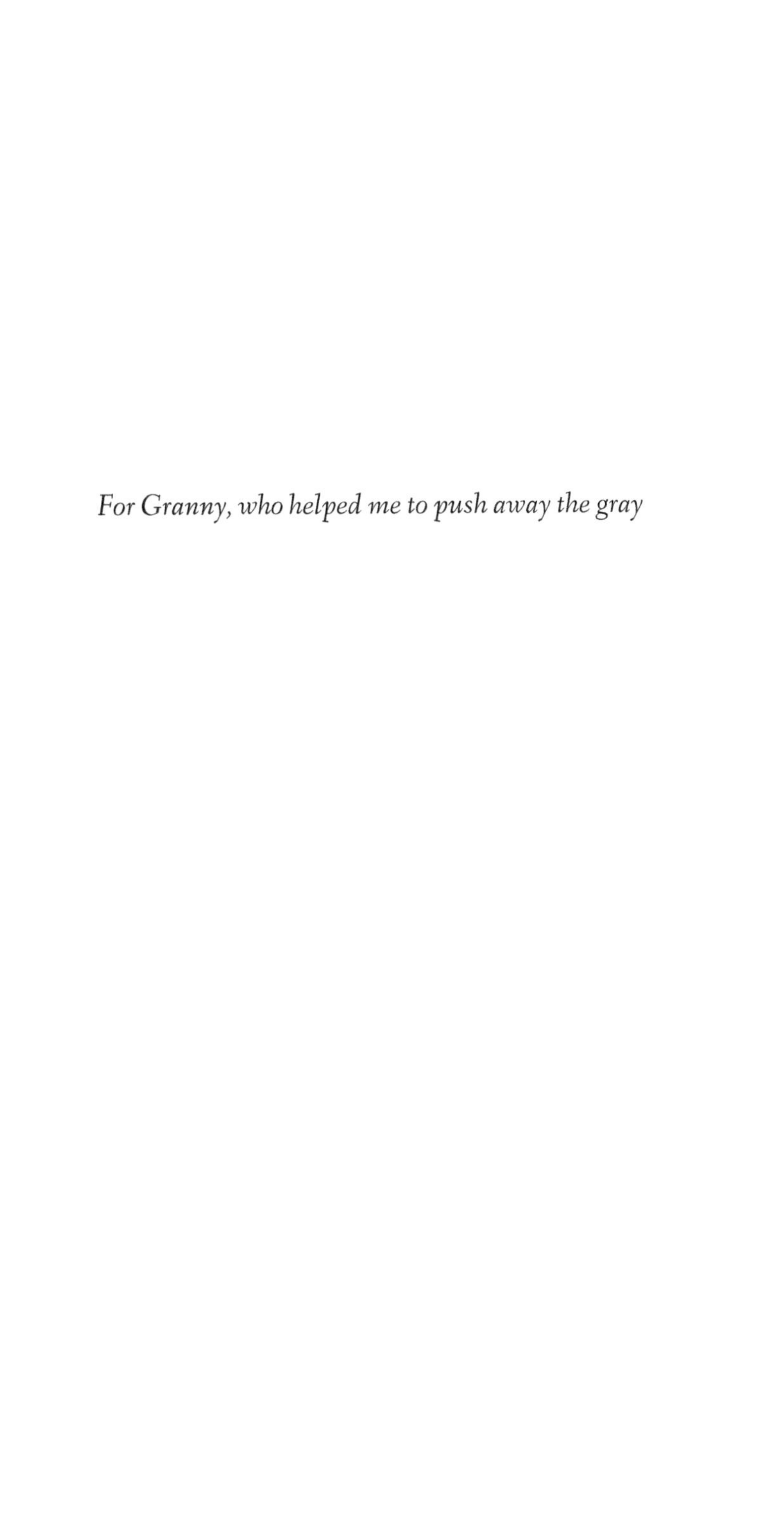

For Granny, who helped me to push away the gray

THE HOUSE THAT JOHN BUILT

"IT'S NEARLY YOUR TIME," the sickeningly perfect voice almost sang.

"But—" the young man began, his voice gruff and gravelly in contrast to hers. The blood drained from his face until he was pale and ghostly, his new and inescapable reality hitting him like a rod of iron. *This can't be,* he thought, the muscles in his body tensing as if preparing to run.

"All try to hide, Emmett. But none are able." Standing

there in a white toga, a golden belt wrapped around the waist, the Priestess' gaze fell on him. Eyes piercing through Emmett's, she seemed able to read his every thought and fear. "Take your gift and use it wisely."

Opening his mouth to speak, Emmett's throat became dry as a desert. He couldn't say a word, and it felt as if he'd fallen into a nightmare. *Only, I can't wake up from this one. And soon, I won't wake up at all.*

"Here," she said, holding out her hand, offering the gift nobody wanted. And yet, there wasn't anything to do but accept it.

Reaching out, his warm palm brushed against her icy hand, and Emmett took the ancient gold piece, contemplating. *I guess this is how my kin felt when receiving their own tokens ... I always wondered.* Resolve hardening, he asked, "How long do I have?"

Smiling politely, she paused thoughtfully. "Long enough to utilize that." She nodded at the golden piece in his hand. "I will come for you when it's time."

Before Emmett could say more, the woman turned and retreated the way she came, silky black hair falling down her back.

Exhaling, Emmett released a breath he'd been holding to the point of gasping. As he looked once more at what rested in his hand, he shook his head. Then, continuing down the road, he kicked a rock or two that rested in his path. And, even in the face of death, he felt a pang of guilt upon remembering how much his mother had despised the habit. *Poor woman was always trying to break me of it.*

One foot in front of the other, he walked, finally reaching the small log cabin he'd built with his own two hands. Entering, he carefully placed his toolbox on the shelf, wiping away a little sawdust. Fingers resting on the hammer Emmett's father had given him, he pulled it from the wooden box, handling it tenderly. *Things change so fast,* he thought, considering how he'd spent his day woodworking . . . before the life-changing meeting with the Priestess on the road.

Emmett eyed the empty rocking chair, table, bookcase, and bed he'd crafted in the hopes of sharing them one day. But the opportunity had never come. Returning from labor to the warm and loving arms of a wife had never been his lot. Nor had his dream of rosy-cheeked children at his wife's apron strings come to fruition. Instead, he was greeted by a cold hearth and empty bed.

Fury building up inside, Emmett looked down at the gift in one hand, hammer in the other. Slowly, he gripped them harder and harder, knuckles turning white, as he once again thought of his lonely, meaningless life. *Vagabonds will take my home and things – nobody cares that I lived, or whether I die.*

Emmett drew his arm back, as he powerfully flung the hammer forward and across the room. It spun through the air, the polished metal glinting as it caught the last light of the day. Smashing into the river stones of the fireplace, a chunk of broken rock tumbled from the hearth along with the hammer. First cringing at the damage, Emmett's expression quickly turned to rage. "Why should I care?" he shouted at the empty room. "Nobody else does!"

Letting out a sound somewhere between a grunt and a yell, he rushed toward the hammer. With one swing of his leg, Emmett sent it smashing at the chimney once more.

Staring at the cloud of soot he'd knocked loose, he gripped the token tight, hating to accept the thing the Priestess called a gift. Eyes searching the room, he knew it was the only thing left in his life that held any true value. *But what am I supposed to do with it?*

Emmett stumbled toward the rocking chair and allowed himself to fall into it. He rarely sat in the chair – it was to be his future wife's, and he wanted to keep it as perfect as possible for her. Now, the sentiment seemed incredibly foolish. "I could have been sitting in comfort all this time," he growled aloud. "Not a single woman sat in the thing!"

Wincing, Emmett remembered his words weren't quite true. One woman *had* sat in the chair. "I thought she was happy here," he whispered, thinking of the charming conversation and her sweet face. Running his fingers along the arm of the chair, Emmett thought of Lucy doing the same, admiring his work and filling him with hope.

"John had more money, though," Emmett said, his voice sounding like the death that would soon visit. Memories came, threatening to overwhelm him as he thought of the lovely face that had lost its joy over the years, the happiness starved until it was dead. It had been unbearable to watch, unrelieved even by John receiving his own token.

Had Lucy chosen Emmett, he knew their life would have been simple. Walks along the shore, conversations by the fire, and daily adoration would have been their prizes. Mouth tight in a grim line, Emmett muttered, "Security of possessions won over security of love. It *couldn't* have been worth it."

But, even as Emmett belittled what her choice had brought, thoughts of John's magnificent home, the baby that was almost as beautiful as her mother, and the carriage and fine things Lucy owned flashed through his mind. Much as he hated it, the debate was easily won. There were too many ways it had, indeed, been *worth it*.

Running a hand through his dark hair, Emmett's heart

sunk, tightly gripped by remorse. Unable to handle the onslaught of memories any longer, he stood without knowing where to go. *But I* have *to leave this empty house – I can't stay another minute.* Anger burning inside, he took long strides to the entryway. He slammed the door behind him and slipped the token into his pocket.

At first, he seemed to walk without purpose. The beauty of the sunset momentarily distracted him from his short and uncertain future. *Mother always loved to watch the last of the sunshine paint the sky miraculous colors,* Emmett thought. He slowed to stand in silence, remembering that her golden piece had been used to fill her last moments with the lavish colors of the dying sky.

The colors turned, and as soon as the golden and fiery-red rays turned to pastel orange, purple, and blue, Emmett once again felt the weight of the gift in his pocket. And his steps turned.

Picking his way carefully, staying in shadow to reduce town gossip that spread like wildfire, Emmett moved along. He considered the weight of various choices he could make with the last bits of his life. And the heavy consequences of not fighting for Lucy slowed his steps.

As if paralyzed, he finally stopped beneath a tree. There it was — John's beautiful house with the only woman Emmett had ever loved somewhere inside.

Although he usually found a way to avoid the place, when he didn't, he couldn't help the rush of feelings that made him want to run in and break Lucy free from her prison. And at that moment, the same feeling came. Emmett suddenly knew he'd been foolish to not see her before. "Why did I wait until the time of my death? The exact moment when seeing her would bring me peace and joy while causing her such deep pain?"

Inching forward, Emmett's heart wanted to be with Lucy and succumb to selfishness. But as the last light of the sunset disappeared, and the stars began to shine more brightly, something stopped him. The tinkling laughter of a child trickled over the sound of the waves that crashed behind the house that John built. And then, he heard Lucy laughing with her little girl. *She sounds so happy.*

Shaking his head, heart heavy, he knew and accepted that the last and best thing he could do with his life was not add to Lucy's suffering. Turning, Emmett deliberately made his way to the rocks, boulders, and sand that led to the lapping water of the ocean.

Kicking stones once more, Emmett thought of his life and vain pursuit of happiness. *I tried so hard and, in the end, my efforts were fruitless, with always yet one more lesson to learn. But with death at my door, what were all the lessons and toil for? I never gained any of the joy I sought.*

Unwilled, his head turned to look back at the putridly perfect house that John had built. The beautifully lit home that kept the only thing he'd ever wanted, yet failed to acquire.

The waves lapped, attempting to soothe the wounds of his soul with their patient coming and going. But, instead of comforting, to Emmett, the sound was incessant and grated at his brain. Or perhaps the aching annoyance came from the fact that his mind had fallen to pondering past failures.

It was more than he could bear to look at John's house a moment longer, his mind feeling torn and raw from past and present choices. He knew he had to walk away. Turning his head once again, Emmett walked toward the ocean that tortured him, hoping it was a less painful view.

Slowly walking, his feet came to the hard-packed sand. And a moment later, a sound teased at his ear – one he thought could only be his imagination. *I* would *imagine that at this moment, now, wouldn't I?* A grim smile forced itself on his lips, and he bent over to pick up a stone, wiping the sand away.

"Emmett, is that you?"

This time, it was more difficult to blame his mind. And the sound of footsteps that sunk into the sand made it even harder.

"Emmett?" Came the lovely voice that always brought intense pain from the loss of it in his life.

As soon as her soft hand gently touched Emmett's arm, the anger within seemed to melt, and it took every bit of willpower to not sink into her arms. Looking down, the name he had tried to keep out of mind escaped his lips, low and gentle. "Lucy."

Looking at her — eyes bright and shimmering under the full moon — Emmett was filled with regret for every moment he'd wasted before and after John's death. Like a pig-headed gentleman, he hadn't fought the way he should when Lucy chose John. The way Emmett would have, had he known what lay ahead. *And had she still chosen John, I should've run to Lucy after his death, offering the happiness she deserved.*

But now it was too late.

Lucy's pure, sweet face tilted upward. "It's lovely to see you, Emmett. But why are you here?"

Standing on the cold sand, the waves crashing, Emmett didn't know what to tell her. Perhaps Lucy was expecting to hear something about night fishing or searching for seashells. *Maybe she's hoping I came to call on her.* For Lucy's sake, Emmett wanted to come up with some reason that wouldn't give away the token in his pocket. *But I have no such response.*

Instead, he had a mouth empty of words. Unable to speak, against better, prior judgement, he reached into his pocket and pulled out the mockery of a gift. Hand open, he held it out to her, the ancient gold gleaming in the moonlight.

Gasping, Lucy covered her mouth, her face becoming drained and pale. "No, Emmett . . . *no.*"

His voice grew as strained as it had been when speaking with the Priestess. "She gave it to me this evening."

Lips trembling, Lucy threw herself into his arms, their bodies close and comforting. Wrapping his arms around her as tightly as he dared, Emmett pulled Lucy in, breathing in the flowery scent of her hair as he rested his head on her shoulder.

Emmett couldn't force himself to do what he knew he should – protect Lucy and remove himself from her life. And so, clinging tightly to one another, they remained in each other's arms as they mourned.

Slowly becoming aware of his indulgence and its possible consequences, Emmett tried to brace his mind, preparing to remove himself from her arms. He wouldn't have ever let go, but at the thought of the returning Priestess, Emmett knew he wasn't the only one to consider.

Pulling away from Lucy felt like tearing his own flesh, but he knew it had to be done. *I can't stay. It would just add to her pain.* And yet, he knew he couldn't die with words left unspoken. "I should have come sooner, Lucy. And I should have never let you go the first time —"

"I chose wrongly, and I've regretted it every day," she said, the words rushing out of her mouth. "I wanted to come to you — to see if we could mend things. But I didn't know how you could forgive me. Emmett, I can't tell you how glad I am that, even if it's just a moment, you came to me now." Moving closer, Lucy opened her arms once more.

The struggle deepened as Emmett wanted to give in and accept the love he'd always hungered for. But the weight of the token reminded him of the emotional debt it would leave behind. And Lucy would be the only one left to pay it.

"No, Lucy," he said, stepping back. "I can't do this to you. You've already suffered too much. I – I won't add to it."

The expressions that washed over her face were many, but the final one that came and remained tortured him most. *Pain.* Even though it was the last thing Emmett wanted for Lucy, he'd brought it to her, anyway.

"I see," she said in a voice little more than a whisper. "I shall miss you, Emmett. Very much."

A little sob escaped her lips while one hand covered her mouth, and the other reached out to stroke his arm. For the last time.

Turning, Lucy walked away, shoulders shaking with grief.

The waves shredded across Emmett's ears like nails down a chalkboard as he watched her go. Heart pounding, guilt crashed over him. Emmett hoped he'd die from the pain that was growing in his heart. Because he knew every one of Lucy's next steps would be even more devastating to watch than the last.

Unable to bear the agony of seeing his beautiful Lucy walk away, he ran after her. "Lucy, wait. Lucy!"

Steps faltering, she turned.

"I'm a broken man, Lucy," Emmett said, grasping her small, soft hands in his rough and overused ones. "I don't know what's right or wrong. I want to be with you every last minute I have — it's all I've *ever* wanted. But I couldn't do that to you. It wouldn't be right. When the Priestess comes, I —"

"Then let's spend every last minute together, Emmett," Lucy said, cutting him off. "It's all I've ever wanted, too. I will always be heartbroken at my loss and stupidity for not choosing you . . . but at least I won't also have to bear the burden of *this* regret."

Stepping closer, he placed her arms around his neck. He then took Lucy around her waist. Leaning down as his heart pounded, Emmett's lips met Lucy's. And he kissed Lucy as he'd always wanted. Soft, sweet kisses that made him feel more alive than he ever had. Tender kisses that made him want more as her mouth bewitched him.

Brilliant stars dangled from above as the lovely scent of the salty air mingled with the spicy perfume Lucy wore. Both of which intoxicated Emmett as they held each other close.

Finally separating, they walked up to the back garden, hand in hand. There, on a bench swing, laid several blankets. Plucking them up, Lucy sat down and said, "Come, Emmett. Sit by me."

Smiling, he approached her, then sighed, joining her on the bench. Lucy tucked into his side, covering both of them with the warm quilts.

Rocking and swinging on the bench like a ship at sea, they talked and looked up at the stars. They spoke of loved ones, regrets, and her child — the only joy in Lucy's life. They talked about everything, except for the ancient token, even though it kept their mouths and hearts open.

Comforted in each other's arms, the night deepened, and their eyelids began to lower against their wills. With Lucy's hand tucked into Emmett's and resting on his chest, Emmett fell asleep to the sight of her lovely head on his shoulder. And he drifted off to the sweet sound of her breathing.

Beautiful things never last long enough, though, and Emmett woke much sooner than he would have wished. The thing that woke him wasn't as pleasant as the thing that had put him to sleep. The voice of the Priestess calling churned the acid in his stomach.

"Emmett, we must speak."

Opening his eyes, Emmett sighed — there she was, waiting. And not simply part of a nightmare. "Is it time?"

"Yes," she said, a note in her tone leaving Emmett uncertain of how she felt about bearing the news. "And your token — what have you decided?"

For you to disappear, Emmett thought, his initial reaction gruff. It was all too real, and he didn't *want* to say – it would only add to the reality. But he knew that silence wouldn't solve his problems, nor could he make such a request for a disappearance. The Priestess and her sisters were still there, so they must have survived past similar requests without vanishing.

"Yes, I've decided," he said, his voice rough. Aware of the token he'd despised and considered a curse, he suddenly knew it was something of a gift, after all. *It made my last moments spent with Lucy more precious than the rest of my life. I hadn't seen the value in choosing what to do with the last hours until I held Lucy in my arms.* "I'm using my token to stay with Lucy a little longer. And I'd like you to retrieve the rocking chair I built. But please come back to me before it's time – I don't want to die here. I want to be far away from anyone."

"I can do that, but . . . you don't want to spend the last of your life with Lucy?" the Priestess asked, curiosity on her face.

Emmett wondered at her questioning. It occurred to him that she spent little of her life with the fully living, and infinitely more time granting last requests from the nearly passing. It was likely that most of them didn't want to leave their loved ones before their death. *I crashed back into Lucy's life, though. It would be better for her if I simply vanished.* Emmett knew she didn't need anything more to deal with than the already-mountainous grief.

"This is my wish," he whispered. Reaching into his pocket, Emmett found the cold, heavy token and handed the ancient thing over to the woman who was just as timeless. "Please."

"It will be as you wish." There was a quiet moment while the Priestess looked at the token. Tucking it into a purse at her hip, she finally nodded. "I will return with the chair."

Emmett lost track of time as he stayed there with Lucy, the moments they rested together precious and sweet. And it brought sharply contrasting bitterness when the Priestess returned to take him Home.

Carefully placing the rocking chair next to the bench swing, Emmett gently tucked the blankets tightly around Lucy. Then, emotions welling within, he embraced and kissed her once more, grateful she stayed asleep.

Touching the arm of the rocking chair, then brushing Lucy's sweet cheek, Emmett turned to the Priestess. "I suppose I'm ready."

She led the way back down to the driftwood, rocks, and waves of the ocean. Footprints pressing into the sand, Emmett wondered if Lucy would see them in the morning and whether she would follow along in an attempt to find him. *I hope not.*

Mind wandering as he walked, he was curious if she

would remember the chair. *I hope she'll be happy to have it.* In a way, it was like leaving his embrace for her to have whenever Lucy needed it.

He took footstep after footstep, weary and grief-stricken, torn about wanting relief and what that truly entailed.

"I know it must be hard for you now," the Priestess said after they'd walked longer than Emmett thought he had strength for, breaking the silence. "But you will be happy when you are Home."

Pursing his lips, Emmett considered her words. He supposed it was her way of trying to comfort him, but it was a failed attempt. As he took those last steps of his life, Emmett thought, *Even Home can't make me happy.*

"There, you'll wait for her," the Priestess continued, making him wonder if she could hear his thoughts. "Time moves quickly when you're Home. And soon, Lucy will be in your arms. For eternity."

Turning to eye the Priestess, Emmett considered her words as his thoughts shifted. *I will be happy, someday. When Lucy and I are together once more.*

"We're far enough away now." Her deep and all-knowing gaze seemed to pierce through Emmett's eyes once more. And her next words brought an unsettling chill to his bones. "Are you ready? It's time."

Emmett knew he wasn't, but there was nothing more to do. Closing his eyes, Emmett thought of his night spent with Lucy before he answered, "I am."

They stood still a moment, the wind pulling at their clothing, both waiting for death to arrive. And though Emmett had said he was ready, as it creeped closer, fear gripped him, and he realized just how ill-prepared he'd been.

Gasping for air, Emmett cried out, stumbling forward into the Priestess' arms that struggled to help him to the ground. And as his life was ending, Emmett saw the Priestess look at him in alarm. In that moment, he understood her hesitancy in accepting his wish for her presence at his death. Because it didn't only pain him.

As Emmett felt the blood in his body slow as his heart stopped, one last thought flashed through his mortal mind. In spite of the ugliness and pain of death, the image of lovely Lucy came, and he remembered how it felt to be in her arms.

A wave of peace washed over Emmett, and he knew he could patiently await at Home if it meant an eternity of being with Lucy.

THE HANGING TREE

THE TREE CREAKED every now and then, whispers coming from its branches as the boughs conversed with the passing wind. The woman standing several feet from the tree listened, her loose curls tossed gently in the breeze. But she couldn't understand the many secrets they shared with the choppy river that rushed along nearby.

Amid yellowing leaves, raindrops that fell from dark, angry clouds, and moss that seemed to strangle and cling to everything in sight, the woman made out the objects her eyes sought. Eyes focusing, she looked at the foreign objects that hung on the limbs, dangling like gruesome versions of ornaments hung on Christmas trees.

"So many . . . too many," she said, her voice low.

Slowly swaying in the wind, many laces that appeared eerily similar to nooses tied empty shoes to boughs, long-departed from the bodies that had once worn them. Appendages that would never adorn such things again.

The woman's mouth drew tight, fists clenching, the fingers of one hand turning white as they gripped the objects of her own secret.

One step after another, she walked closer to the trunk, despising its existence. Yet, even as her being filled with hatred, she felt compelled to move toward it. Unwilled, she raised a hand, fingers outstretched and reaching while memories assaulted her mind.

As screams and blood-splattered images raged in her head, she caressed a pair of filthy, faded red shoes. And seeing intruding moss, spiderwebs, and decomposing leaves that covered them, the woman's heart tightened.

She dropped the burden she'd been bearing and took hold of the shoes. Clawing at the moss and grime, the woman's already-stained hands became covered in the muck, the debris forced deeply and painfully beneath her nails.

"Why?" she screamed, trembling as her fingers slowed, brushing away the last of the filth. Tears forming at the corners of her eyes, flinging her arms out, she shrieked at the tree, "It should have been me!"

Body heaving as deep breaths moved in and out, she stood and stared at the tree once more, wishing she could smash the thing into the river behind it.

Breaths calming, the woman's mind returned to her

purpose. She touched the faded red shoes once more, carefully untying the laces and pulling the shoes down from the limb.

"You don't have to worry anymore," she whispered more quietly than the trees, cradling the shoes as she spoke to them. "He can't hurt you anymore . . . or anyone else."

Carefully, she set them down on fallen, yellow leaves. Then, eyes narrowing, the woman picked up the secret-ridden objects she'd brought along. Companions that served only one purpose — to adorn the tree in place of the faded red shoes.

First one, then the other, she tied them to a branch, almost snapping the laces as she yanked the knots tight. And as she did so, more recent thoughts entered her mind. The difference was that remembering *those* violent screams and blood held satisfaction.

Her work finally done, she stood back. Looking at the morbid new ornaments, a grim smile touched her lips.

Inhaling deeply, her chest rose, then fell as she exhaled, one emotion overcoming the rest — *closure.*

Once again, she picked up and tenderly held the red shoes that, day after day, had faded on the bough of the tree. Shoes that should have never hung there at all.

A new memory imprinted on her mind, and the woman turned, finally ready to walk away forever. And as she did so, her eyes caught sight of a deep red, glistening drop as it slipped down one of the newly-hung shoes. Moving slowly, leaving a trail of scarlet behind it, the orb fell to the ground below, splattering against a fallen yellow leaf.

Inspiration for The Hanging Tree

Sometimes I write to find relief from emotions and life. Other times, I'm so moved by a conversation or image, a story blooms in my mind, almost without my control. The Hanging Tree was inspired by a friend telling the attendees of a book club – myself included – about a tree with all kinds of shoes dangling on the trunk and branches.

Now, I've seen such trees before, but the way she described this one was decidedly creepy. Even more disturbing, however, were her expressed thoughts along the lines of, "What happened to the owners of the shoes? That many people can't just leave their shoes out there in the woods by the river. Something must have happened to those people."

As you can imagine might happen at a book club, this sparked a whole lot of speculation that wove in and out of our conversation throughout the night. And when I was driving home, I couldn't shake the eerie feelings I had when thinking of that tree with its mossy, spider-web-laden shoes. Nor could I ignore the seed of a story that'd been planted – I didn't hold out more than a day or two before sitting down to write "The Hanging Tree."

In case you're wondering, yes, I went to visit that tree. I dragged my family out to see the thing, and my husband kindly agreed to take photos of it. Standing there beneath the boughs, looking at the shoes that are so quickly being taken over by the elements, I found myself wondering the same things as my friend. I've come to the conclusion that Bonnie's description rightly captured the creepiness, and you'd never catch me out there at night.

BUT NOT ONLY FOR ME

The first steps on the beach,
Have come from my own feet.
The sand, washed smooth and clean,
Seems there, solely for me.

But as my feet indent,
My mind becoming spent,
I think of every soul,
That'd walked along the shoal.

Many had walked on that sand,
With full or empty hand.
Some with eyes of tears,
Both young, and full of years.

Perhaps there to say goodbye,
To ones sent off to die.
Or gathered under the sun,
To celebrate vows of love.

Looking at the sunrise,
With more understanding eyes,
I walk a little more,
Along the ocean shore.

Seashells come and go,
But this one thing I know;
The sand is smooth and clean,
But not only for me.

THE GHOST THAT WORE ROUGE

YOU NEVER KNOW how scared you'll be of a ghost until you meet one.

Jesse had heard those words from the time he was a little boy and — until recently — had secretly been petrified of finding out. He'd grown up, though, no longer thinking of ghosts. Sandy blond and tall, he had a few extra muscles to spare. And more good looks than he deserved, on top of the rest.

He supposed the town rumors of the ghosts and excessive superstition originally came from the old Miller place. Some said the ghost of the long-dead Mr. Miller spent near every night by the well where his daughter fell in and drowned. When Jesse was young, it made a whole lot of sense to him, and figured that's what he would do, were he in the same predicament.

And, of course, there was the Forgotten Woman's house, too, which didn't bring peace to his innocent and fearful mind. His hair near stood on end at the thought of her sitting there, rouging her lips all night long, hoping a man would come to call. And he'd rather do extra chores than let his mind wander to what it must be like when the woman moaned and wandered the house near dawn when a man didn't call.

At some point, though, he had grown up most of the way, and the pretty smiles and figures of girls muddled his head. It never was quite the same again. Although, it's sometimes hard to tell if the brains of *any* young men unmuddle quickly after their teen years; so there's a good likelihood that what happened was *not* exactly Jesse's fault.

Dancing had gotten things off to what he considered was a fantastic night, which wasn't necessarily such an evil. There was, however, more than one red flag he should have taken note of. But then, Jesse's head was a bit scrambled from the beautiful girls and their twirling, fancy dresses cut a little lower than everyday gowns.

The finer-than-usual drinks at the public house didn't help, either. Though he usually kept his hands *mostly* to himself, the liquor tended to make them bold. Those wicked hands had gotten him a good stomp on the foot during more than one jig, and most certainly deservedly so.

Jesse probably could have ended the evening as he usually did — shouting a few rowdy *hullos* in front of the preacher's home, then throwing a rock or two at his windows for good measure before taking a quick stroll back to his quarters. That is, he *thought* he was throwing rocks at the preacher's windows. In reality, Jesse was usually too drunk to see straight and was lucky if those stones made it past the picket fence.

That night was different, though. Maggie was at the ball. And if Jesse had ever been sweet on anyone, he'd been sweet on Maggie.

Usually, Jesse was on his best behavior around the woman. He even tried to cut back on his intake of strong drinks when she was in the vicinity. The night of the incident, however, Jesse had downed several glasses of this and that, taking dares from friends, when the girl of his dreams arrived fashionably late. And by then, it was too late to hope for any good behavior.

"Maggie," he whispered to himself, squinting a little to get a better look and clear his drunken vision. "Your red lips are divine."

Most likely, it was just rouge and not divinity, but Jesse couldn't tell the difference in his intoxication. The band starting up once more, Jesse thought it a perfect opportunity to ask for a dance. Taking a few lumbering steps in Maggie's direction, forcing what he considered to be his most charming smile, his heart beat in time with the music.

"Miss Maggie, you're lookin' mighty fine t'night," he said, bowing low and trying to keep his balance as he reached for her hand. Only, the alcohol had altered his eyesight a bit more than he'd realized, and Jesse ended up grasping at air.

Giving more grace than Jesse deserved, Maggie took a step forward, holding out her hand for him to take. "Why thank you, Mr. Jacobs," she replied, her lovely red lips drawing up flirtatiously. "Now, I thought we'd dance when I arrived, but you've spoiled my fun. You're too drunk to see straight, and I won't have you trampling over my new shoes."

"New slippers, now. That's just fine, Miss Maggie. How 'bout I take a look?" he asked, one hand catching her skirt and pulling it up a bit before Jesse could remind himself to behave.

Blushing and showing signs of both fury and intrigue, Maggie smacked his hand away. *Hard.* "That's *enough,* Jesse Jacobs. I won't be dancing with you *one beat* tonight." Turning on her heel, ringlets bouncing, she was about to go when Jesse snagged her wrist and whipped her back around.

"Please, m'lady. I promise I'll be good from here on out," he said, pulling her close and looking down into her deep green eyes.

"Well . . . if you swear," she said, hesitating and looking at him with eyes that were just as sore for Jesse as his were for hers.

"I swear," Jesse whispered, his speech a little more slurred than usual.

"Fine, then. I'll dance with you once. But that's *it,*" Maggie said, pretending to be more upset than she really was.

"Then that's settled. Let's jump in now," he said, taking her hand and dragging her out to the floor a little more roughly than he realized.

The next moment, they were stepping in time, circling, and wildly swinging through all the right steps. And even though he could barely walk when drunk, there was something in the liquid that made Jesse dance like no other.

Which was probably why Maggie agreed to it after he'd gotten fresh with her.

A few more spins and a little footwork brought them to the end of the dance. Taking a more controlled bow than the one he'd offered upon greeting his dance partner, Jesse took Maggie's hand once more, trying to keep her from escaping. "Miss Maggie, come outside with me to get a little air, please — I've got something to tell you."

"You don't say?" she replied, eyes widening and cheeks flushing as she followed him to the door. "I suppose that'd be all right."

Out in the moonlight, those rouged lips were even more tantalizing than ever, and Jesse pulled her out of the busy front garden toward the back. Walking toward the river that glittered with star and moonshine, Jesse searched for just the right spot. Finding a tree that cast just enough shadows for discretion, he pulled Maggie close as he stepped beneath the boughs.

"So, what did you want to tell me?" she asked, long lashes batting teasingly.

"A few things," Jesse replied, touching one of her curls. "I wanted to tell you that you're pretty . . . and sweet," he whispered, pulling her in closer than Maggie's mama would have ever approved. "And . . . I want to give you a kiss."

Jesse thought that *looking* at Maggie made his heart crazy. But kissing her did unspeakable things to it. Inches from her lips, he realized she smelled like honey and flower petals. And when his mouth met hers, the softness was indescribable. At first, he kissed her gently, savoring and enjoying everything about Maggie.

Maybe things would have been all right, had Maggie let one little kiss by the river well enough alone. But she didn't, and that's when the trouble began.

Rising up on her tiptoes, Maggie wound her fingers into Jesse's hair, then pulled him even closer than *he'd* dared. Some say Maggie even wrapped one of her legs around Jesse's. Passion thick between them, their lips and mouths moved wildly. And that's when those evil hands began their mischievous work.

They went this way and that, doing all kinds of things they shouldn't while a moan or two escaped Maggie's lips, encouraging even more wicked behavior. Had Jesse been sober — and not so muddled — even *he* wouldn't have likely approved of his hands' rotten manners that seemed to be attempting to explore a few too many inches of Maggie's body.

Now, even though Jesse had chosen a fine enough hiding spot, brothers tend to know things. Like where *they* would go if they wanted to neck with a girl. Maggie's brothers were no different. And they noticed when their sister was missing.

Occupied with what his hands and lips were doing, Jesse didn't hear a thing. Uninterrupted, he would have kept right at his business. But those three big boys almost simultaneously smacked the back of his head, threw a good punch in his ribs, and yanked Jesse away from his Maggie.

Landing hard on his rear, Jesse was shocked. Though the preacher would have never approved of his activities that night, it wasn't necessarily the most Christian way to put an end to the situation. And Jesse wasn't in the least bit happy about it.

Scrambling to get to his feet, drawing his arm back to take a swing at one of the brutes, Jesse saw one of those brothers taking Maggie away, while the other two with near more muscles than him circled Jesse.

Normally, Jesse would have had a fair chance against the two boys. But unlike the dancing, drunkenness made him a poor fighter. And so, swing as he might, his aim barely made its mark once or twice before the brothers licked him good. Maybe he wasn't quite hollering for his mama, but one eye would be solidly black in no time, blood seemed to be pouring out of his nose, and Jesse was certain a rib was broken.

"Have you had enough, Jacobs?" the oldest brother with the chipped tooth demanded, staring down at him from above. Lying on the ground, Jesse nodded, wishing he'd never gotten involved with Maggie — her red lips weren't worth this type of beating.

"Good. Now stay clear of our sister," the other said, glaring at him and getting in one last kick to Jesse's stomach for good measure. "Get on your way, boy."

Rolling over, grunting in pain as he did so, Jesse stood up, wiped his nose on his sleeve, and stumbled away. Steering clear of the front of the building where he might cause a scene and ruin his reputation with the ladies, Jesse tried to not pay any mind to the brothers gloating about their victory while he was still within earshot.

Sheepishly making his way to the road, Jesse headed home on his usual route, staying in the shadows whenever he could. Reaching the preacher's house, a lot more angrily than usual, Jesse grabbed a few rocks from the ground. Having had the snot knocked out of him, the intoxication seemed to have been unrattled a bit, and his aim was more true than normal. One, then two stones hit the front windowpane.

Happy with his better-than-usual arm, Jesse was just about to throw another rock to smash the glass in when footsteps pounded throughout the house before the front door was flung open. Cracked rib or no, he took off running for the cemetery beyond the house.

Enrobed in darkness from the mature trees that grew throughout and around, he had no trouble sneaking off to Big Bill's tombstone that was as large as the nickname sounded.

Chuckling to himself as he thought of the preacher's angry face and striped nightcap, Jesse waited until he was certain the man had gone inside. "Probably will give a fine sermon on Sunday about loving thy neighbor," he muttered, holding in a guffaw.

When all was quiet and the lights finally went out at the preacher's, a good amount of time had passed. Squinting through the cemetery, knowing he'd have to weave carefully through the thing to pass the preacher's house without waking him, Jesse determined his best exit. Heaving himself from the ground where he'd been sitting above Big Bill's remains, some of the pain of his wounds came rushing back.

Stepping with care, head down, Jesse made his way to the road once more, looking back at the house to double check he wasn't being watched. Certain it was safe, Jesse turned around, ready to scurry home as quickly as possible. He'd made too many enemies that night, and things needed to blow over before he met any of them again.

Instead of the empty road before him, though, not too far from where he stood lurked the most gorgeous woman he'd ever had the pleasure of laying his eyes on. Leaning against a fencepost, she wore a revealing overcoat that complimented the dark and sultry gown draped over her fine figure. And the red rouge that glistened on her lips made Jesse's head spin.

"Well, hullo, there, Miss," Jesse said, sauntering closer.

"You sure are a sight for sore eyes. Especially to a fella down on his luck."

The smile that showed her pure white teeth urged Jesse on.

"It sure is late. May I escort you somewhere?" he asked, holding out his arm.

With a flirtatious shrug, the woman stepped closer, daintily taking it. Being as grungy and filthy as he was, Jesse was glad it was dark enough to hide the blood, bruises, and dirt that had to be covering him.

"So, where are we headed, m'lady?" Jesse asked, using his worn-out charm. The girl didn't say anything, though. Instead, she simply nodded up the street.

While he was used to a gal who liked to talk quite a bit, Jesse didn't mind and spoke enough for the two of them. Half of it was smooth talk, the other, stories about his many skills and strengths that weren't remotely close to truths. It didn't really matter to Jesse — they puffed up his ego, whether they were false or not.

Stopping in front of a lovely cottage he'd never noticed before, the woman let go of his arm and slowly turned down the path that led to the door. Turning to look at him, seduction on her face, she waved her hand, beckoning him to come. Looking at that red rouge, clinging gown, and welcoming face, Jesse gave in to temptation and hurried to catch up with her on the walkway.

Taking his hand and giggling, the woman pulled Jesse inside, closing the door behind him. Never having been in that type of situation before, Jesse didn't quite know what to do with himself. While the woman went to the kitchen to put the kettle on, he looked around at the lovely gold and porcelain trinkets that sat on the mantle and caught a glimpse of the bedroom.

"This is a fine place you have here," Jesse called, pretending not to watch as she next moved through the bedroom doorway, leaving it open for him to see. Though the cottage wasn't the largest, everything was stylish, from the candlestick holders, to the linens and sofa. And he'd never seen such a fine four-poster bed with a canopy that gently moved with the early autumn breeze. "All kinds of nice things . . ." he muttered, eyes widening as she unbuttoned and slipped out of the snuggly-fitted overcoat to show her slender, smooth shoulders. And everything the dipping neckline exposed. The next moment, pulling up her gown a little, she eyed Jesse and winked at him as she nudged off her slippers while Jesse gulped.

What Jesse saw next nearly sobered him, his heart raced so quickly. The woman unbuttoned her dress, eyes fixed on Jesse the entire time, then let it slip to the floor around her feet, exposing the thin, revealing slip she wore underneath. Finally, she turned to the mirror, sat down, and took down her hair, slowly drawing a brush through it.

"Come," she called a moment later, voice soft and smooth as silk, filling him with fire.

Slowly sauntering into the bedroom, Jesse's heart had never pounded harder. Quiet, he watched the woman in that low-cut, clinging bit of an undergarment as she dabbed perfume on her arms and bosom, then picked up a little container that held red rouge.

"I've been waiting for you a long time," she said, eyes on the mirror.

Now, as you'll recall, Jesse had gotten himself stupidly drunk that night, leading him to the moment when he found himself in a beautiful but strange woman's bedroom chambers. And practically naked at that. Watching the lady in front of the mirror, something was odd about the picture.

Had he not been *quite* so intoxicated, Jesse would have figured it out sooner. But the alcohol and whipping from those two blokes hadn't done him any favors.

Still, to his credit, Jesse forced himself to ignore the seductive woman. Instead, he tried to puzzle out what was the matter as she applied what was becoming an excessive amount of red rouge to her lips.

Unable to decide what it was that bothered him, Jesse looked around the place once more. And instead of seeing fine things, this time, his eyes revealed a vision that made his hair stand on end.

The trinkets on the mantle weren't expensive at all, as they'd appeared to be moments before — they were worn, chipped, and covered with cobwebs. Cocking one eyebrow, Jesse noted that the whole place was in horrid disrepair, with fabric on the furnishings that had disintegrated, and a chair toppled over with one of its missing legs lying on the floor nearby. Where he'd seen the most fashionable drapes just moments before, he now found rags trembling against shattered and dust-covered windows. Most disturbing to him — perhaps due to his previous high hopes — was the beautiful four-poster bed canopy that had turned from sheer white to a few yellowed strips that clung to the rotting wooden rods.

Fear creeping in, he turned back to the woman at the tattered dressing table and finally understood what was wrong. He felt as if a bucket of ice water had been poured down his back.

There wasn't a reflection looking back at the woman as she continued to rouge her lips. No, not one at all in the chipped mirror above the now-empty rouge tin.

And that is when Jesse Jacobs found out how scared he was of ghosts.

Heart beating wildly, gasping for breath, he was petrified. The Forgotten Woman slowly turned to look at Jesse. "Don't go," she whispered, sending a chill up his spine that made his skin feel electrified.

Without waiting a moment longer, Jesse tore out of that old house a changed man. Or changed *into* a man, one could say.

Though nobody saw Jesse Jacobs for a solid few months, folks 'round town noticed he began visiting the pastor instead of throwing rocks at his house ... and fence. And he never touched a drink again, that anyone saw.

Even more, he began checking in on his widowed mama more than once or twice a year when he needed some funds. He visited near every day, taking her flowers every so often, and sitting down to listen to her neighborhood stories, or happenings with the ladies' group at church. Most noticeably, however, was the fact that he paid attention when his mama told him the kind of woman Jesse *ought* to be after.

Nobody really knows whether Jesse Jacobs ever would have changed without seeing that ghost. But, years later, happy in a home with a good wife his mama approved of and three children, he shuddered to think what he might be like and whether he'd still be the same without the vision of the Forgotten Woman.

Most folks probably would have stayed away from that old cottage if they'd seen what Jesse did. During the day, Jesse never avoided it, though — it kept him humble and on the straight and narrow.

However, during the evening, Jesse made sure he wasn't anywhere near the thing. He kept a strict curfew and was at home in the arms of his flesh and blood woman. Because he intended to never see a ghost again.

Especially not one that wore rouge.

The Legend of Xtabay – Behind The Ghost that Wore Rouge

If I weren't scared of creeps, cliffs, and cougars, I'd take a solitary hike every day. As things stand, I'm afraid of dealing with those things alone in the middle of nowhere, so I generally hike with my family, which also rocks. No pun intended.

I've only ever been on one hike I truly despised — four miles of trekking through a mosquito-infested swamp is NOT my thing. One good thing came of it, though. Our family told stories as we hiked — an effort to keep our minds off the bloodsuckers.

Working our way through the sludge, my husband told us the legend of Xtabay, the ghostly Mayan woman of incomparable beauty that lured men out into the forest. After living a life of pride and passing judgements, never showing kindness, the woman died. Full of regret, she persuaded evil spirits to bring her back to life so she could have a chance at love. Because of her wicked heart, though, her revival only returned her in the form of a ghost.

To this day, she desperately seeks love, often seducing unfaithful men away from bars and down a path that leads off into the woods.

Inspired by the tale my husband beautifully retold, I wrote my own version of Xtabay in a whole new setting. Because, folks, that Jesse Jacobs boy is decidedly Southern.

COMING BACK

Coming back is never quite just as you thought
  it'd be,
Unchanged land and childhood friends will not
  wait there for you.
Instead, you'll find the unfamiliar, and also
  forgotten glory,
And where there once were fruit trees, a sky of
  unhindered view.

Open and so vulnerable, both land and soul will be,
Mind enlightens — all has changed without your
having granted.
You'll wonder why you ever returned, to find those
hewn-down trees,
Where once, so young and innocent, their roots in
fresh soil planted.

Although the world around has changed and
brought a saddened tear,
We, too, have changed, experienced, and grown up
as a whole.
Coming back, it's hard to do, and often full of fear,
But if we don't, we'll never find the anchor of
our soul.

PETTICOATS AND SPLINTERED BEDPOSTS

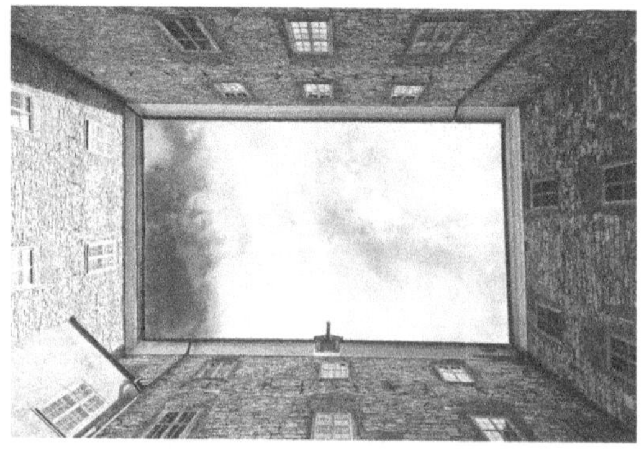

NO DOUBT ABOUT IT, Sheriff Joe had been suspicious. However, seeing Annabelle with the snapped and splintered bedpost that dripped with blood solidified things real quick.

Stomach churning, Joe looked at Annabelle's dead beau awkwardly draped across the bed. *No good ever comes from a stormy night like this.*

"It's not what you think," Annabelle whispered,

breaking the silence that'd only been interrupted by the sounds of rain and wind howling through the window.

Cocking an eyebrow, Joe adjusted his badge. "Miss Annabelle, this looks to be *exactly* what I think."

"There was a woman —" she argued, dropping the bedpost.

"Miss Annabelle, this here is a *small* town," the sheriff said, interrupting as he put a hand in his trouser pocket. "Ain't too many suspects. Seein' as you're here . . ." Voice trailing off, he shrugged before pulling out a handkerchief. "Here. Clean yourself up."

As much as Joe wanted to hear her story — most women wearing their finest things didn't end the night by beating their beau to death — he couldn't have a crying woman on his hands. *It'd make me go right soft, and that's just plain unacceptable.*

Annabelle protested, wiping her bloodied hands with the handkerchief while Joe kept an eye out for evidence. *Nothin' here but signs of a struggle between these two. Except for this,* he thought, picking a piece of lace from one of the splinters.

"Sheriff!" his deputy called, dragging a clawing, hissing saloon girl into the room. "I found her sneaking out the window."

"I didn't do it," she cried, yanking herself free as a rumble of thunder shook the house. Breathing heavily, she glared at the dead with disgust in her eyes.

Holding up the evidence, Joe's eyes widened. "Your lace begs to differ."

Cheeks turning red as her scandalous petticoat, the saloon girl angrily spat on the body. "He had it comin'. He told me . . . he didn't want our baby."

ALONG THE OCEANFRONT

HER FOOTSTEPS FOLLOWED the sound of the waves crashing against the shore. Wiping away tears that fell without permission, Annie wasn't sure how a person could be so full of joy one moment, and the next, completely filled with despair. It seemed impossible.

Yet, that was her exact experience the moment Hanson's brother had whispered to her.

Annie knew the way she'd left the table was unsightly — his entire family gathered around the table, finishing their meal and about to open Christmas presents. But she couldn't sit there a second longer. Catching Hanson's gaze after Mitch's whispered secret had said it all. Watching his uncomfortable glance turn away from Annie and toward *her* direction — the childhood sweetheart Annie secretly hated — Hanson looked at Mitch once before turning to meet her eyes, and Annie knew it was true.

"I can't believe I wanted to marry that jerk," she said loudly, relieved when her bare feet met sand. Thinking back through the months, it suddenly made sense why he hadn't proposed. "But why bring me here — to humiliate me in front of his family? So I could get a good look at his *real* future wife?"

Even as she muttered to the crashing waves, tears still falling, Annie knew he wasn't as bad as that. "Hanson probably just felt bad about telling me right before Christmas . . . he knows I have a hard time being alone this time of year."

Reaching the hard-packed sand, she walked along in the light of the full moon until she reached a driftwood log and sat down. She watched the crashing waves when the full body sobs came. Dropping her head into her hands, Annie didn't fight it. Instead, she embraced the cries that forced their way out, hoping their release would bring some bit of relief.

"Three years!" Annie shouted into the wind, all too aware of the idiocy of shouting to the ocean like it could talk back. But this was the tipping point. "I wasted three years of my life with that creep."

After years of searching, she thought Hanson was the one. He'd been an obvious choice to everyone in her life, and the way he made her feel was indescribable. "I should have *known* things were taking too long — he obviously had doubts that should have been red flags to me."

But his caring, sweet, and considerate nature made her feel secure. Deep down, she'd sincerely believed he was committed. "How does someone do that – talk about marriage, children, career choices, and vacation plans based on a relationship," she said, running a hand along her forehead. "Then start seeing a high school fling behind their girlfriend's back?"

Thinking she'd been having a private conversation with the ocean, Annie was surprised when Hanson's deep voice came from behind her. "I'm not seeing anyone behind your back, Annie."

Flipping around to look at his gorgeous face that was slightly shaded by scruff, she found him to still be as sizzling as a cologne ad model. If only she wasn't still so taken with him. But he *cheated* on her. She had to regain control. "Mitch told me he saw you two at the beach. He said you were cozy and holding hands . . . that you were spending a lot of time together before I showed up." Annie's eyebrows drew together, scrutinizing the man before her. "And that you kissed."

"Before storming out, did you ever consider that Mitch might be wrong?"

A bucket of water doused her inner fire, and Annie admitted to herself that she hadn't. There was so much history between Hanson and Kara, it just made sense – Annie felt she was the backup plan. Still, she supposed he was right, and maybe it hadn't been fair of her to jump to conclusions. But she had to know. "Well, is he?"

For the tiniest moment, Annie thought the whole thing had been a nightmare that was about to dissipate. *Maybe it was all a misunderstanding, and Hanson has an explanation.*

The moment was ruined, however, when Hanson

simply shoved his hands in the pockets of his jeans. Looking away from Annie, his mouth pulled into a tight line, and the expression screamed, *guilty*.

"You know, Hanson —" she began, her voice low and quiet, feeling as furious as the moment Mitch had spoken to her.

"It hurts, Annie, that you would believe my brother before me. I thought you knew me better." The pain in his voice cut her like a knife.

"I . . . I *want* to believe you would never do anything to hurt me, but you aren't denying it. And, well, I guess it makes sense that you would ultimately choose her." Annie thought of the tall brunette sitting at the table for Christmas dinner, making eyes at Hanson. She'd thought it was ridiculously desperate when Hanson was so clearly taken. Until Mitch had shared. "Besides, my father taught me that *anyone* can have second thoughts . . . at any time in a relationship."

"Annie, I'm not having second thoughts, and Kara doesn't have a single thing on you — I don't know why you can't see that. But you standing up at the table and saying those things was embarrassing." He stepped closer, brow furrowed. "If you would have come to me, I would have told you the truth. Since you didn't, though, I'll tell you now." He sighed and ran a hand through his hair. "Kara's mother died last week, and she's at home for a bit to help her father. Growing up next door, of *course,* we've seen each other pretty often in the last few days."

Hanson was quiet, rubbing his jaw. Taking a deep breath, he continued. "When we talked the first time, it was all about her mother. She cried, and I couldn't just stand there. I patted her back and gave her a hug, but I *swear,* I didn't feel anything other than brotherly toward her. The next day, she caught up to me when I was jogging on the beach. I thought there was something weird about her vibe – she seemed to be feeling my status out," Hanson said, scratching the back of his neck. "But I talked about you the whole time . . . and my plans with you. Kara said she was happy for me.

"Last night I was out here, and Kara came and found me again. I was quiet and listened about her mom some more." Cringing, he rushed on, apparently eager to get the next words out and over with. "The next thing I knew, she took my hand, and then she tried to kiss me."

Each word made Annie feel like the air was being squeezed out of her lungs.

"I'm guessing that's what Mitch saw — from up there, in the dark, it probably looked like we *did* kiss. But I didn't let it happen, Annie. I got out of there. Because I love you, and *nobody* has ever made me feel the way you do. And nobody has ever loved or cared for me the way you do."

Confused, Annie turned to look out at the sea. With the waves coming toward them, she didn't know what to believe. What Hanson said made sense, but so had her father's lies. Until the other woman showed up on their doorstep. "Why didn't you tell me when I arrived, Hanson? And why was she at dinner?"

"I chewed my mom out for a good long time about the invitation — she was trying to be nice to Kara with her mom passing and didn't know what happened last night. And I didn't tell you, because I didn't want to ruin tonight . . . I have a gift I wanted to give you later, but I'm thinking now would be best. I think it'll fix this mess."

"Hanson, no gift is going to fix this — we need to talk—"

He sat down next to her and wrapped his big, strong hand around hers. "I've never understood why you think you're second class compared to everyone else, Annie. I guess it's probably because of your father leaving." He tenderly stroked her hand. "To me, though, you're the most gentle, loving, thoughtful, fun, adventurous, and gorgeous woman I've ever met. I've always wanted a wife and children, but until I met you, I couldn't see it happening with anyone I dated."

Although a part of Annie wanted to keep a wall of protection around her heart, she knew Hanson's words were sincere. And she couldn't help the fact that they melted her, washing away the anger and confusion.

"I want you to be my wife and the mother of my children, Annie. You're my best friend, and I'm completely in love with you." Pausing, Hanson pulled something out of his pocket and slipped down onto one knee. Holding out the most beautiful diamond ring of intricately designed rose gold, Hanson continued, "Please, Annie. I can't imagine having any kind of fulfilling life without you. I love you and want to be with you every minute I can. Will you marry me?"

Suddenly, the argument seemed ridiculous. Looking into his eyes, Annie saw hope, love, and a sincerity that had never been in her father's. And without Hanson, her heart would be an empty shell. Because she was in love with the man.

"Yes," she said, smiling through tears of joy as he slipped the ring on her finger. "I couldn't imagine my life with anyone else, either. And I love you, too."

Standing, Hanson took Annie's hands and pulled her up. Annie looked into his eyes, and the world was suddenly a glorious place. Stepping closer, Hanson drew Annie into his arms. Annie's body tingled with warmth as she took in the masculine scent of his cologne that mixed with the salty ocean air. Hands moving up and down her back, Hanson pulled Annie in even closer, his warm breath tickling her ear and sending a shiver down her spine.

Annie's eyes met Hanson's once more – his gaze piercing and full of longing. A reflection of her own. Lips slightly parting, Annie held her breath. With a low groan, Hanson leaned down, pressing his lips to Annie's.

The waves crashed below as their hearts pounded, lips moving together, each unsatisfied with the idea of separation.

And as they kissed, Hanson's arms tightly around her, sweet happiness washed over Annie. Whatever came their way, she knew they would be able to make it through. Hanson was all hers, and Annie knew her life would be complete with her soulmate.

ENROBED IN GRAY

THE AUTUMN DAY when the endless months of rain began always made her feel the same — as if she lived in black and white, instead of color.

The gray had a way of seeping into everything, from saturating the soon-empty boughs of trees, filling the sky above, and soaking through every pore of her skin, settling deeply into her bones. It dulled her mind and prevented sprouts of creativity, let alone blossoms. The gray told the woman that nothing was of value, be it effort or pastime. It even whispered that emotions — from love to hate — were a waste of energy.

DRIP, DRIP, DRIP. From the first drops that fell from heavy-laden clouds, she knew what awaited on the road ahead. They soaked into her skin like a toxin, poisoning her soul.

Wielding invisible weapons, the woman fought off their spells. Seeking light, laughter, and imagination, she struggled to see the colors.

But she was one, and they were many, and they refused to quit their onslaught. Slowly, the colors faded, giving in to enrobing gray.

And her world was dark.

The rays of the sun didn't extend their friendly morning welcome. The air was stifled with perpetual humidity, speaking of its plans for decay, and refusing to allow fresh breath for her lungs. And each time the door was opened, drops fell in an impenetrable sheet, daring her to step outside.

Eyes and feet heavy, the woman trudged through the gray.

Days, weeks, and months passed with only glimpses of light to give hope that was quickly destroyed. Surrendering, she gave in, and her soul's fire was devoured by the gray and endless drops.

Only survival kept her heart beating. Mind numb, she forced her body to move through each day. At times, there was no way to discern between the ticking of the clock and the dripping of the rain, but she didn't really care. She couldn't, in the gray.

It seemed there was no end.

She was trapped. And there was no chance of escape.

Yet, one morning after many, something other than rain

awakened her. Slowly at first, the sun poured life in through her window. Then, the long-awaited elixir — the only thing that could win the battle — came in full force. Finally, its warmth forced out the gray, dried out the world, and rekindled the light of her soul.

When her eyes opened, there was beautiful, bright, vibrant color all around. Her landscape was once again full of hues that brought happiness. Her heart beat with excitement as her mind became lively. An ancient, relieving sigh escaped her lips.

And she was alive.

IT CALLS ME

SHE HAD no more and no less than she needed. At least, for that day. Sometimes, Adelia had less. Those days didn't really bother her, though – she had become used to deprivation.

Standing up from the log that had washed ashore long ago, her always-bare feet sunk into the sand as the fishermen began to leave for home. Adelia had gotten used to the deep sadness that threatened to be overtaken by jealousy as she watched them return to loved ones in the village each night.

She knew what awaited them – children with rosy cheeks who would clap and squeal to see their fathers, and apron-wearing wives who would gladly kiss their husbands because they knew they were fortunate enough to have them returned home safely. *I would have done the same . . . had I been given the chance.*

The last of the men gone, her only companion left was the sound of the ocean. Turning her head downward, Adelia smoothed her humble apron and skirt, then pushed the thought aside, replacing it with a new one. *I* will *do the same.*

Taking a deep breath of the sea air, she tucked a stray, black, wind-whipped lock of hair back, then began carefully placing trinkets, woven grass bowls, and jewelry into her basket. Smiling a little as she looked at her handicrafts, Adelia once again appreciated what the beautiful oceanside afforded to those who lived there. The little shells, grasses, and driftwood were the perfect mediums for her craft and were proof that the ocean and its surroundings were generous. Sometimes.

Adelia tried to forget the times when it was brutal, greedy, and treacherous. But that was a difficult task. All day, waiting beside the ocean as she sold her things, she was reminded of her loss to the massive beast the ocean was.

The ocean knew how good he was – how beautiful his smile, how blue his eyes. It had *to try to take him.* Turning to look out at the vastness that stole her Jacob and daily surrounded her, Adelia's resolve strengthened. *It will see. Someday, the ocean will know that he is stronger. They will* all *see.*

Turning away from the water as she did every night, Adelia walked up the path that led toward her hut. She stepped along more slowly than usual, her mind resting on a memory from earlier in the day. Brow furrowing, Adelia thought of the little girl who had come to buy fish and stopped for a treasure from Adelia's basket.

Though Adelia knew that the villagers mostly bought her things because they pitied her, if they stopped to listen, she would tell them stories. She wasn't surprised at the generous gifts they traded when her bartered items included a tale or fortune. Her words might be the only thing that broke up the monotony of their weekly work. And it might be the story that would bring them attention and laughs when sharing it as their own while gathered around a fire with friends.

She knew they ought to give her credit for the tale. But more than an acknowledgement, Adelia wished that she was welcome to join them — to partake of their happiness.

It doesn't really matter, she would tell herself when the wind brought the words of one of her stories told as somebody else's. Mostly, they were just silly stories of things she'd witnessed in the village that nobody else had; Adelia knew that if one would sit still as long and as often as she did, a myriad of curiosities would often pass by.

And the villagers knew Adelia watched. The women came to her for love advice and to hear the latest gossip with discretion — they knew Adelia would never make a peep about their inquiries. While the men didn't usually bother with romance or gossip, they knew she watched the tides and sun more closely than anyone. Perhaps due to her lost love, they listened to her. Of course, they'd never acknowledge her advice with more than a nod, but on days when she warned of bad weather, the men stayed home and mended their nets.

Continuing along the path to her home, Adelia spotted her hut ahead, standing dark and all alone, away from the rest of the village. Sighing, she didn't want to go inside. *It's so lonely there.*

As she looked at her humble home, Adelia remembered a question a little girl had asked that day . . . along with her answer. And with the same brutal force as the waves of the ocean, the memories of the night that Jacob didn't return crashed into her. Breath catching, devastating memories of the battered boat and solemn faces swarmed in her mind, bringing so much pain, she gasped for air.

"Why do you come here every day?" the beautiful girl with golden locks had asked when the sun hung directly above their heads.

Taken aback, Adelia paused, bending down to pick a long piece of grass that was growing nearby. Playing with it as she considered her answer, Adelia patted the spot next to her, inviting the young girl to sit. Working the grass until it became soft and flexible, she pulled a heart-shaped shell out of her basket. "Because . . . it calls me, Heidi."

Pausing, the little girl picked her own piece of grass and mimicked the young woman by which she sat. "Why does it call you? My mama says he won't come back," Heidi responded, looking innocently at Adelia.

Surprised that Heidi was so bold, Adelia once more carefully thought about how she would answer. Slipping the shell onto the supple grass, she gently took Heidi's hand and tied the simple bracelet around her wrist. "Because I know his voice is mixed with that of the ocean's. And it calls to me because he makes it speak for him. And in return, I call him back. You see, they are fighting a great battle. But I know my Jacob will win." Smiling prettily as a young woman should, Adelia patted Heidi's hand. "I don't mind if your mama says he won't come back. She's probably forgotten how strong Jacob is. But we know better, don't we?"

Nodding soberly, Heidi looked at her pretty new bracelet, fingering the lovely shell. "I hope he wins soon."

"Me, too," Adelia had replied, then motioned for Heidi to run along, knowing that the family of her young friend was too poor to offer Adelia anything in exchange for the shell. "Run along and help your mama get dinner. That'll make her happy, and your papa, too."

"Yes, Adelia. And thank you for the beautiful bracelet," she replied, bowing her golden head a little before walking away a few steps. Hurrying back, Heidi whispered, "I'll crunch some extra egg shells in your garden – to keep the slugs away."

"Why, how generous of you, Heidi. Thank you," Adelia said, imitating the little girl's confidential tone.

"You're welcome," she had said, then scampered off toward home, leaving Adelia to watch her and think about their conversation.

Breathing deeply in and out, Adelia looked up at the vastness above. With the stars beginning to dot the darkening sky, Adelia looked back once more at the ocean, wondering if watching it from dawn 'til dusk could actually will her Jacob to return. Finding it difficult to hope, Adelia turned and walked the last steps to her threshold.

First putting her basket down inside, she wandered through the garden that offered most of her meager sustenance when the weather was kind enough to allow food to grow. She smiled to see that egg shells had been strewn among the plants that mostly came from bartering for seeds. Choosing a few vegetables, Adelia picked her way back, running her fingers along the shell-and-driftwood wind chimes that were strung along her roofline.

Opening the door once again, Adelia sighed as she slowly moved inside, placing the garden goods on the tiny makeshift table that held a basin and pitcher, serving as Adelia's kitchen. She walked on the rough, driftwood boards and planks that made up her floor and sat on her straw-made bed, looking at the fireplace. Digging in her apron pocket, Adelia pulled out a biscuit she'd wrapped in a handkerchief; a token she'd exchanged for a few bone needles earlier that day.

It almost seemed to melt in her mouth as she nibbled it, savoring every crumb. However, even though she was grateful for it, Adelia couldn't help but find its appeal lessening as she ate. The small pleasure it brought disappeared with every bite and much too soon, it would be gone.

Not wanting to bother with building a fire, Adelia simply washed the vegetables she'd picked, then slowly ate them raw. She didn't necessarily eat because she enjoyed them — they certainly weren't like the biscuit — but because they gave her health.

Holding a root vegetable out in front of her, Adelia looked at it, wondering why she should trouble herself with eating it at all. *I've eaten the same things nearly every day for so long, I can't remember when I began.*

Eyeing it more closely, she thought about what the families in the village were doing and what they had eaten for supper, whispering to herself, "It's likely that they didn't sit in the cold, eating *this.*"

For a moment, a vision of her future came to Adelia's mind like a wave rushing up the beach. She imagined the years that had preceded continuing — unchanged — for many more into the future, the pain pressing onward as she daily hoped and prayed for the return that she so patiently awaited. *They think I'm foolish to wait — they whisper that I should move on. But they don't understand. How* can *they when the love they've known is infantile in comparison to what we shared?*

She was strengthened in her resolve for the smallest moment, but it wasn't enough. Doubt tugged and pulled at Adelia once more, dragging her deeper into the thoughts of an empty future. She envisioned herself sitting on a piece of driftwood with her basket day after day as she aged and withered like the grasses she wove.

Holding the vegetable, squeezing it tighter and tighter, Adelia felt a sudden and complete despise for it. Unable to force herself to eat yet another unwanted bite that would give her the strength to live another day without her Jacob, Adelia stood. Shaking with anger, she screamed, thrusting the food away from her and into the fireplace as hard as she could. Face twisted in pain, Adelia remained standing, breathing heavily as she faced the hearth that gave no warmth.

Unbidden, Heidi's face came to Adelia's mind, and a wave of guilt washed over her as the little girl's sweet innocence seemed to beg her to find a way to hope. Usually, Adelia could gain strength from such a memory, but tonight, she was defeated. Sighing, she whispered, "I shouldn't have lied to her."

Walking over to the hooks on which she hung her humble clothes, Adelia unbuttoned her dress, letting it fall to the ground. Taking her nightgown from its peg, she pulled it on, not troubling herself with hanging up the attire on the floor. *It won't be the first time I've worn a wrinkled dress. Nor the last.*

Feet pressing into the driftwood floor, she was only slightly comforted when she climbed into bed, pulling the blankets up. Though Adelia usually considered her bed to be the one constant luxury in her life, tonight, it only reminded her of how absolutely and completely alone she was. And the nagging cold refused to allow her to forget.

Closing her eyes and trying to fall asleep in such a highly volatile state only reminded Adelia of the night so long ago when she'd tried to use slumber as an escape.

Remembering how happy Jacob was the morning he'd walked away from her for the last time was bittersweet and brought with it the unfaded memories of what had happened afterward. The day passed without incident for Adelia, while far out in the ocean, her worst nightmare had come to life. Unwilled, Adelia lay cold, once again imagining the water clawing and batting at the large fishing boat until Jacob was taken captive by its waves. Rolling over, she tried not to think of how disturbing it was to know that she'd gone about her day as usual while Jacob was tossed overboard and pulled out to sea.

Along with the other women of the village, Adelia had gone to meet her love that night. One by one, the boats came in, and kisses were given before the couples walked away until finally, the captain brought in the boat on which Jacob fished. Each crew member got off, soberly and pityingly looking at Adelia as they moved past her, taking off their caps and bowing their heads. She could still taste the acidic bile that built up as they had done so. When the captain slowly appeared, eyes full of remorse and shaking his head, Adelia felt as if her soul had instantly died.

Tossing and turning once more, Adelia remembered the day, nearly a year later, when she stood all alone to greet the boats. She was waiting and watching, refusing to give up hope for a return of her love. Although they didn't say so, Adelia knew that *she* was the reason for the discontinuance of the tradition. The display of her grief made them uncomfortable. And the women believed that waiting would bring the same curse upon themselves that Adelia suffered. Perhaps they were right; perhaps it was the ocean's way of keeping them fearful and cautious. *I don't care what they think,* Adelia had told herself. *I will wait every day. And he will return — I know it.*

"What a fool I was," Adelia growled, slamming a fist into her pillow. "I should have never hoped. I should have *never* told myself those things — that he had lived and would come back. They were lies!"

The pain that had been growing in intensity somehow expanded even more, and Adelia felt her body begin to shake as she gasped for air. Abusing her pillow again and again as she was overcome with emotion, Adelia let go of what she'd been holding back. Unleashed was the mounting darkness and despair of many days that had been held back only by crumbling hope.

Tears flowing, Adelia was haunted by every regret. Each day she'd sat by the ocean and waited while the villagers had slowly begun to believe her senseless. Every time she told herself the same story she'd told Heidi. And, most of all, her choice of allowing Jacob to get onto the fishing boat that day. *Why? Why was he taken from me?*

Thoughts cycling over and over, undimmed visions boldly alive in her mind, Adelia was tortured. And there was nothing to be done, no relief to be had, because Jacob was gone and always would be.

With dark thoughts and the bitter cold as her companions, Adelia exhausted herself. Finally, she was lulled to sleep by the sounds of the ocean drifting through her home, the waves crashing against the rocks on the shore below.

And as she fell asleep, Adelia hoped for the peace that could only come from never waking up again.

A noise awakened Adelia from her deep sleep. Eyes blinking open, she thought a shutter must have come loose and was banging in the wind. Standing up and pulling a blanket around her, Adelia became aware enough of her surroundings to see that the windows were latched closed. Realizing that a villager must be at the door in the middle of the night, she suddenly wondered what was wrong. Hurrying to the door, she opened it, ready to help with whatever disaster must be occurring.

But a villager wasn't standing there – it was a man she didn't recognize in the earliest light of dawn. Opening her mouth to speak — to ask why he was there and what he wanted — Adelia quickly snapped her mouth shut, the words having been torn away from her lips by the sudden shock she felt.

Though older, his body having filled out in the peak of masculinity, face aged and somehow even more handsome, Adelia knew exactly who the man was.

Rushing forward, the blanket dropping behind her, Adelia threw her arms around Jacob's neck, holding him in an embrace that might have been considered violent if it wasn't intended to be overflowing with love.

Jacob held her just as tightly, reprieving her of every desolate feeling she'd had since his disappearance, squeezing and pulling Adelia into the warmth of his arms, as if he wanted their bodies to fuse together. It almost hurt, but she didn't care. It meant that Jacob was there and that he was real — that his love was once more surrounding her mind, body, and soul.

Without loosening the grasp of their arms, Jacob's lips found her ear, cheek, forehead, nose, and mouth. He kissed her over and over, then pulled her in tightly once more, nestling his head into her neck as they cried together.

Whispering into his ear, Adelia finally spoke. "How are you here?"

Pulling her even closer than Adelia had thought possible, Jacob answered quietly and simply. "I heard you calling me."

Tears mingling as their skin touched, their faces close, Adelia breathed, "This is a dream." Lifting her head to look into his eyes that were as deeply blue as the ocean, fresh sobs shook her body. "I can't bear its ending, Jacob."

Passionately placing kisses on every inch of her face once more, he whispered in her ear, "It won't end . . . I'm here. And I won't ever leave."

La Novia del Mar – The Lover of the Sea

There's some debate about how "It Calls Me," the short story, was inspired by the legend of La Novia del Mar. I remember my husband telling me about a time when he'd seen an older Mexican woman who sold things along the shore. As I recall, she claimed her love was lost at sea, and she was waiting for him to return. However, my man claims he simply told me the legend of La Novia del Mar and never saw such a woman.

Another tidbit of inspiration came from a song my husband loves and translated for me by the band Mana. "El Muelle de San Blas" is its own lyrical take on La Novia del Mar. In this version, people believe the woman to be insane because she waits and watches, always wearing the same dress so that – should her love return – he will recognize her.

To add to the conflict, after some research, I discovered

that sometimes the story includes a young man who is a sailor, and other times, he's a pirate. At the time that I wrote "It Calls Me," the sailor stood out to me, though I might have to rewrite it with a pirate at some point. Scribbling it out with that twist could be quite intriguing. Especially if I can imagine him as a younger, sober Johnny Depp type of pirate.

Either way, the tale, images of the beautiful sculpture on the beach of Campeche, Mexico, and my first recollection of the story were all inspiring. And, in the end, it doesn't really matter. So long as it's keeping the legend alive. Below, you'll find the story as I remember my husband telling it.

Long ago, during the days when pirates were rampant in Campeche, Mexico, the ocean and a young woman spent every day together. The ocean loved her and thought her more beautiful than any other who visited its shores.

The young woman liked the ocean and came to walk along the sand, smiling as the waves shone and sparkled just for her.

Watching ships come and go, she looked out to sea. She was curious and always wanted to know more about the people who visited her home.

One day, a young sailor came to port, immediately falling in love with the gorgeous young woman. And she, in return, fell in love with him, giving the sailor all the smiles she usually saved for the ocean.

Watching their love bloom, the ocean waited jealously as the days turned into weeks. Though impatient and biding its time, it knew the sailor would be called to sea once more.

And one day, he was.

Grief-stricken, the lovers were separated, the young man promising to return. While watching her sailor depart, the lovely girl's tears mixed with the waters of the sea, and the jealous ocean lapped at her feet in an attempt to comfort.

Unable to console her and full of envy, the ocean sought revenge.

Raging in its deepest waters, forcing waves high and strong, the ocean wrestled with the sailor's ship. It thrashed and beat upon the boards of the watercraft, finally getting its way. As the ocean pulled the young man into its treacherous depths, the sailor struggled to break free from the crashing waves. But the ocean was too strong. Soon the young lover sunk to his watery grave.

The woman never knew what happened to her sailor. But she knew their love was so strong, he would return.

In vain, she waited. Days, weeks, and months turned into years that passed just as the previous ones had. And she walked the sand, watching the waters, smiling unknowingly at the jealous ocean that had taken the life of her lover.

AT THE CROSSROADS

At the crossroads, I have gazed
A time or two in my few days.
I've often wondered what would have been,
Had choice moved me toward the other end.

But once again, the crossroads I see,
A decision full of treachery.
And only I will ever know,
If the trail has brought me to Joy or Woe.

On my left, an unknown path,
Misted over, yet free of wrath.
But searching down upon my right,
A crumbled road, dark as night.

On the right were Hate and Fear,
To be my friends through all my years.
Anguish, Scorn, and Jealousy,
I knew my companions would always be.

And also, there to be my friend,
Lady Lonely, would take my hand.
She'd lead me off to many places,
Without ever stopping at loving faces.

All alone, and often weary,
Crushing despair, life vision blurry.
Yes, there it is along the right,
The crumbled path that's darker than night.

Full of dread and hoping for more,
I looked to the left as I had before.
And though I once had been uncertain,
To my eyes, had vanished the curtain.

There along the path was Love,
Found on earth and from Above.
Many other friends were seen,
That on the right could have never been.

Kindness, Peace, and Joy did grow,
While Laughter skipped on down the row.
And many a precious soul would I meet,

If I chose to move down that lovely street.

But it seemed two companions I already had,
Were pulling my wrists to the terrible path.
On one hand was Pride, her partner, named Hurt.
They dragged me along, impossible to desert.

I cried out aloud, looking for aid,
But nobody came, and bound, there I stayed.
Moving and inching along toward the right,
I felt my soul growing as dark as night.

Just as it seemed that my fate had been chosen,
My will and my mind so twisted and broken,
Riding with bright eyes and fingers outstretched,
Hope and His sword came to greet this poor wretch.

And when He arrived, I suddenly knew,
With all of my strength, I'd break free from the two.
But looking at Hurt and at Pride once again,
I wasn't so certain they were unwanted friends.

With a plea, Hope desperately tried to persuade,
Begging me come, the two paths to trade.
And there at the crossroads I once again gazed,
Deciding the trail for the last of my days.

Eyes shifting round from Hope to the two,
Torn, undetermined about what I should do.
Surrender to one, and follow the course,
I imagined what life would come from each source.

But unbidden, unwelcomed, the monsters took grip,

Once again wanting my choices to slip,
Down to the path that would have me enslaved,
The road that didn't challenge for me to be brave.

As I walked to the edge, about to go under,
Hope called me again, this time like thunder.
Desperate, untangling, escaping my wards,
I rushed on to Hope with His magnificent sword.

Taking it, swinging, I lashed out at Pride,
Then turned to the other, knowing one more
must die.
Slashing and fighting, I cut to the core.
And then, Hurt, she fell, to rise nevermore.

So full of Flaw, I trembled with fear,
Wondering how, to the good path I could possibly
near.
Then, a new monster beside me came close,
My head bent down low, it was Shame I feared
most.

But Hope came between us and reached out again,
'Twas then that I knew He was my only true friend.
And when I once more saw Hope's fingers
outstretched,
I grasped His strong hand, no longer a wretch.

Then, He and I rode toward the path full of joy,
Free from the monsters that hoped to destroy.
And, though it was hard to discern my true friends,
It was Hope that brought me to Joy in the end.

THE RIVERWALK: A SOULMATE SEEKERS SHORT STORY

"SO, WHAT'S HIS STORY?" Kitty asked, absentmindedly playing with a strand of long blond hair as she watched the man leave their two-bedroom apartment behind the beautiful home on Skyline Drive.

Rolling her eyes, Patricia cringed inside — her twin was pathetically invested. And she tried to push aside a little voice inside that told her she was glad Kitty had missed the meeting. Because she was *just* as invested, even though she would never show it. "The usual. 'Blah, blah, blah, I'm tired of being alone. I want to fall in love with my soulmate.' It's like they all have a script they memorize before walking in the door."

"Patricia, you know you're happy to help," Kitty replied patiently, her tone in exact contrast to her sister's . . . like everything else about the two of them. "Anything else?"

"Well, I guess there was *one* unusual thing about him," she said, tossing back her deep purple hair and throwing on a jacket. "Paul says he already knows who his soulmate is, just needs help convincing her."

"What?" Kitty replied, eyes popping open. "That isn't really the kind of business we—"

"I agreed to help, Kitty. You coming?" Patricia asked, as her long legs helped her quickly reach the door.

"We're *not* using magic, Patricia," Kitty called, hurrying to catch up – their tall, lean body types one of their few commonalities. "That's not what matchmaking is all about."

Making a face, Patricia shook her head. "That's ridiculous, Kitty — we always use magic. And you know it."

"Uh . . . well, not much magic. And *no* love potions. You know how I feel about that." Hurrying ahead and stopping in Patricia's path to block the way, Kitty folded her arms. "Right?"

In something of a stare-off, the twins eyed each other, looking a little like a yin-yang. Other than their personalities being so deeply opposite, Kitty's chic look, lighter complexion, and blond hair couldn't be more different from Patricia's purple hair, darker complexion, and sexier-but-no-nonsense clothing that matched her attitude.

"Of course," Patricia said, breaking the silence. "Now, do you want to help this heartbroken loser, or what?"

"Insufferable," Kitty muttered, then walked around to the passenger seat of their car.

Heading down the riverwalk, Patricia led the way to Frite and Scoop, where she'd agreed to meet their newest customer. While Kitty was holding her grudge against her twin, Patricia couldn't help the grin that spread across her face when they walked up the wooden steps to meet their gorgeous client. *She probably thought I was making him up.* "Good to see you, Paul," she said, voice bright as she caught the scent of delicious, homemade fries.

"Hello, Paul," Kitty said, holding her hand out for the tall, sandy brown-haired man in his twenties.

"Nice to meet you," he said, shaking her hand and offering a charming smile. "Want to sit down? I ordered some frites for us."

"Absolutely," Patricia said, sitting down at one of the picnic tables just outside the door of the hand-crafted ice cream shop — one of Astoria's many gems.

"So . . . Patricia says the woman of your dreams runs past here every day at this time. Point her out when she gets close, okay?" Kitty said, sounding like the uncertain one for once.

Smirking, Patricia was glad Kitty was finally getting a taste of the way she felt every single time they got a new client — unsure and totally foolish. *Of course, it always seems to work out, in spite of the usual craziness. It's amazing how involved those Salem Sisters get with Kitty's little match-making business.*

"In the meantime, why don't you tell me a little about her? Patricia didn't tell me everything." Cocking her eyebrow at Patricia, a pleasant expression quickly replaced Kitty's glare before she turned to Paul. Hands on the table, Kitty waited patiently.

"Well," Paul said, taking a deep breath before diving in. "Rachel and I have known each other since kindergarten. We were always the best of friends. Up through junior high, we hadn't ever fought," he said, reminiscing. "Senior year, it just made sense to start dating because we knew we loved each other."

Quiet for a moment, Paul was definitely living somewhere in the past when Patricia rudely cleared her throat, bringing him back to the table. *Much as I like getting a good look at him, I've got better things to do than stare at an unavailable hunk.*

"Uh, let's see. The whole dating thing was great for a while – I was invincible, and she was cute and fun. We went out on fun dates . . . made out a little," Paul said, smiling sheepishly. "But then, *Jason* came along," he said, making a face. "Rachel wanted to go to the east coast for college, and I didn't. Jason used it as a wedge between us. Told her I wouldn't compromise and would never treat her right."

Patricia looked at Kitty, knowing she could relate. And the pain that crossed her face made Patricia wish that Kitty couldn't understand quite so well as she did. *Poor thing. She'll never get over him.*

"A month into their friendship, we were fighting like cats and dogs, and Rachel broke off our relationship," Paul said, darkness clouding his face as the twins looked at him with sympathy in their expressions. "She wouldn't be friends with me, either. She told me Jason said I wasn't good for her."

The door of the shop swung open, and a smiling, cheerful server approached their table. Apparently noting the serious expressions and silence, she hesitated. Tray wobbling a bit, the teen set the platter of delicious frites and dips down. "I'm sorry to interrupt," she said, then hurried away.

Reaching across the table, Kitty patted Paul's hand. Patricia held back a gag at the sympathetic gesture and grabbed one of the hand-crafted French fries. Glaring at her twin, Kitty said, "That's awful. I'm so sorry, Paul. No childhood relationship should end like that."

"I feel the same," he said, clearing his throat and shaking his head. "The thing is, I've always felt we were deeply connected — like there was something holding us together that nobody else in the entire world shared. I could never explain it . . . it was just something I felt right here," he said, putting a fist on his chest. "I mean, I know you'll think I'm crazy, but sometimes when we were together, it was like we were almost glowing when we were close to each other."

Cocking an eyebrow, Patricia tried not to move a muscle. While humans sometimes accidentally accessed curses, spells, or even spoke to the dead, there were few supernatural talents they were aware of. And seeing or feeling Soul Symbols was one of them. Auras, yes. But the actual symbols, and especially the soulmate symbols that were unique to only two people – the soulmates – no.

Frustrated, Patricia wished she could flat out ask him if he could see the symbols. But the Salem Sisters were a dangerous brood, always searching for reasons to seek revenge for the injustices done to their ancestors and them. There was no need to put Paul in harm's way by giving him information he had no real use for.

"That's a . . . rare connection to feel, Paul," Kitty said, choosing her words carefully. "Um, what happened to Rachel?"

Listening to Paul ramble on about the stupid girl leaving for the east coast, then returning six months ago and turning his world upside down, Patricia took a moment to focus on the aura-like symbols that floated around him. They orbited Paul in beautiful, other-worldly colors, the symbols of his moral and intellectual character almost vibrating. None, however, were as strong as his soulmate symbol — two lightning strikes crossing each other — which burned as brightly as the setting sun.

"So, you're telling me you think she came back because of this connection you both felt. You say it's like a magnet, pulling you together?" Kitty said, eyeing Patricia, who just shrugged the slightest bit.

"I know it sounds nuts, but I swear it's true," Paul said, grabbing one of the frites and shoving it into the Lemon Aioli a little more forcefully than necessary. "Whether you believe me or not, I don't care. I've never felt a pull more powerfully, and if I'd known Rachel would've been happy to see me, I can't tell you how many times I would have purchased a plane ticket and flown across the country. It was a struggle *not* to." Staring at the table, he continued. "Listen, I just need help, and you two come highly recommended. She's the only one for me, and I'm tired of wasting days, weeks, and months without her."

Kitty started to say something, likely making an attempt to lead him in the direction of finding someone else — somebody who was emotionally available. But Patricia knew Kitty wasn't even convincing herself. *Why is Kitty even wasting her breath? Somehow, this man knows. And he isn't changing his mind. Besides, finding soulmates is what we* do.

Paul's head turned to the wood-planked riverwalk, completely ignoring Kitty's trailing words, and it seemed as if time stood still. A woman who couldn't be anyone but Rachel came into view. Tall and thin, jogging in spandex, it didn't take a soulmate symbol to tell she and Paul would make a good match. Rachel's pace slowed as she turned toward them, however, and the spell-casting sisters saw what Paul couldn't — the soulmate symbol that matched his, burning just as intensely. The electricity of every soulmate they'd matched was there, shuddering and trembling in the other's presence. It was as if the crossed lightning bolts were reaching toward each other, vibrating and pulsing, struggling to unite the bodies to whom they belonged.

Heart throbbing for the couple as she watched, Patricia knew she had to take action. Common sense was usually strong with Patricia, even though Kitty often disagreed with her choices. However, at that moment, inspiration struck, and it seemed far beyond the boundaries of street smarts Patricia often liked to use. Even though she knew Kitty would hate it, Patricia knew exactly what had to be done.

Discretely making a sign with her fingers, quickly whispering under her breath, Patricia cast a spell, enticing Rachel to stay there for just a moment longer than she would have. *See? Just a* touch *of magic, Kitty.*

Then, with Rachel still eyeing her high school sweetheart, Patricia turned to Paul.

Smiling, the twin leaned in, wove her fingers into his beach bum hair, and pulled Paul close before he could fight it. Kissing him good, enjoying the task of their lips moving together, she found it interesting both that he was an excellent kisser, and that he wasn't pulling away like she thought he would. Unless he was fighting her off with his luscious lips, an interesting tactic.

Finally pulling away after a good, long kiss, both a little breathless, time seemed to catch up. Satisfied the spell had worked, Patricia looked toward Rachel and tried not to giggle when the woman stumbled over her own feet as she continued on her way.

"Um . . . that was an amazing kiss. And, uh, thank you," Paul said, searching for words. "But —"

"*Why* did you do that, Patricia?" Kitty cut him off, halfway standing up, bumping the table as she did so.

Wow. It's a good thing Paul is here, or Kitty might have pounced on me, Patricia thought, impressed with the aggression of her usually-calm sister.

"That *was* an amazing kiss. Rachel's going to be a lucky woman," Patricia said, winking at him. "Listen. If you want to get her back, you can't just be the same old Paul. That's the boy she dumped in order to travel and follow her dreams. It's the same boy who never did anything and stayed on the Oregon coast his whole life."

"There's *nothing* wrong with Paul, Patricia," Kitty said, grabbing Paul's hand, then making a face and letting go, apparently rethinking even more physical contact with their client. "He's stayed here, yes, but he's wonderful and has made himself into a wealthy business owner," she said. Jabbing a finger at Patricia, Kitty spat, "And if you can't see that, there's something really wrong with you."

"But!" Patricia continued, rushing on to ease the furrow out of the severely confused man's brow. And to get her sister's finger out of her face. "The Paul that's making out with a gorgeous woman in front of a shop is confident, has his life together, and would make *any* woman at least a little bit jealous." Patricia grabbed another delicious frite. Pointing it in Paul's direction, she cocked her head before taking a bite. "Did you see Rachel's face, Paul? Looked more than a bit jealous to me."

Quiet, Paul seemed to be considering Patricia's words when Kitty started to speak. "Paul, I'm *so* sorry. I can meet with you privately, and we can come up with a plan together or—"

"Thanks for the dates, Paul. It's been wonderful," Patricia said, standing up and cutting off her sister. "It'd be a real shame if you broke up with me, but I understand if you have to. Everyone wants to be with their soulmate, I guess."

Just to bother Kitty, Patricia laid a soft kiss on Paul's cheek, then headed down the wood plank steps. "You're a real heartbreaker," she whispered into his ear.

Disappearing down the walk, Patricia hoped Paul wouldn't mess things up — whether he knew it or not, she'd set him up perfectly.

A storm had rolled in, turning the warm air wet and chilly, the waves of the Columbia full of chop. Hurrying along the riverwalk to one of the charming homes on the water, Paul kept his head down. As the rain fell, hair dripping wet, he tried to force out the second-guessing thoughts — a nearly impossible task.

"Maybe I should just turn around and head back to Patricia . . . she'd probably make out with me some more," he muttered, eyes rolling. "I'd likely have more success with that than what I'm shooting for."

Still, he kept on as the winds picked up, over-stuffed drops of rain falling down his neck. Feeling stupid, he kept on, forcing his legs to move until Paul reached Rachel's home. Walking up to the door, he knocked before he could think about it too much more. "Here goes absolutely nothing."

His heart had been pounding before, but as soon as his knuckles hit the door, Paul's heart was racing. Holding his breath, wondering what to say, he waited for his soul mate to answer.

Each second that passed was like torture. Ears on high alert, Paul listened for footsteps. He watched for movement in the house, trying not to be a creeper. But he couldn't see anything, and every scenario he'd imagined was better than his reality because Rachel didn't open the door at all.

Instead, Paul stood there, dripping wet, the words he'd wanted to share trapped inside and desperate to get out.

Knocking again only brought the same result. Letting out a grunt, Paul turned around, allowing his feet to trod heavily as his brows drew together. Leaving the way he came, the last bit of hope was crushed when she didn't fling the door open and call out his name as he retreated. *Of course, she's not there. I'm not living in some stupid chick flick.*

Shaking his lowered head, Paul returned to the wooden planks of the walk. Cold and miserable, each step made him feel worse.

Why did I let myself hope like that? She's never going to know what I feel. Completely absorbed, Paul stumbled into a woman. Cringing at the thought of his big, muscular body crushing the poor girl, Paul caught her arms. He steadied his feet, holding her tight and close, keeping them from falling to the ground.

"I'm so sorry . . ." Paul said, taking a deep breath. And, looking down, there she was, the gorgeous woman he'd always loved. "Rachel." Swallowing, Paul grasped for words. "Uh, I . . . I wasn't looking where I was going."

"It's fine. Totally fine," she replied, eyes shying from his.

Realizing he hadn't let go, Paul let his hands slip down her arms. "Sorry for, uh, this. I just didn't want you to fall, so I held on," he awkwardly explained, noting that she hadn't tried to work out of his unintentional embrace.

"It's okay." The tiniest smile crossed Rachel's lips before

evaporating altogether. "I'm kind of glad you ran into me. It's just, I've always . . . well, I've always wanted to apologize for what happened between us. The east coast — and Jason — weren't half as good to me as you were."

The words washed over Paul, soothing and cleansing the ancient wounds he didn't realize still needed so much healing. "It's okay, Rachel. We were so young."

"Yes," she replied, hesitating. "But I still wish I would have made different choices — those were my greatest mistakes. And now I see you have a girlfriend."

As soon as the words came out, Rachel's face turned bright red. Trying to backtrack, she blurted out, "And I'm so happy for you! That's great — wonderful, really. So, so glad, Paul."

For the first time since Jason had shown his big-nosed face, Paul felt the tiniest portion of hope. Unsure, not trusting what could easily turn out to be false, he didn't know what to do. And he wished the sisters were there to tell him.

"So, um, I'm glad for you, and thanks for being kind about everything. And . . . I'm going to go inside now," Rachel said, her voice trembling with regret.

Heart pounding, still confused, Paul watched as Rachel moved to turn around, slipping out of his life once more. Forcing his mouth open, he quickly said, "I broke up with her."

Feet still, Rachel's expression changed. "Really?" she asked, her eyes seeming to hold the same hope Paul felt inside.

"It was never going to work between us," he said, stepping closer. "Not when I've always known I'm supposed to be with you."

Their bodies close, rain falling around them, they

looked at each other. Closing the gap, pressing her warm body to Paul's, Rachel pulled him into her embrace. He wrapped his arms around his soul mate, relief and love washing over Paul as he nestled into the soft, smooth skin of her neck.

Lifting his head from where it rested, arms still pulling each other tight, Paul leaned down. Like the water of a broken dam, his heart raced. Trying to keep control of himself, Paul softly pressed his lips to Rachel's.

Everything about her was as he'd remembered, only matured and womanly — the bud of a flower in glorious bloom. The memories he'd retained from high school were laughable in comparison to the reality of the warm, loving body of Rachel.

Sweet and perfect, he wanted more of those lips. Pulling her in even closer, Paul kissed his soul mate like he'd kissed no other. And he was amazed at the deep satisfaction he felt when her mouth moved with reciprocating intensity. It wasn't just their bodies that were finally reunited — it was their souls.

A minute, or maybe an hour later — Paul wasn't sure — their lips parted. Taking her hand, smiling and slightly breathless, Paul led Rachel down the wood planks. And, even though rain fell from looming clouds overhead, he was as warm as if rays of sunshine were coloring his new world.

"I've always loved you, Paul," Rachel said, happiness on her face. "I'm glad I get another chance to show you."

Sighing with contentment, he responded simply. "I love you, too."

ACKNOWLEDGMENTS

I've always felt best-expressed through the writing of words. There's something so liberating about it, allowing me to say things my tongue-tied mouth cannot. I'm thankful for the encouragement I've received from friends and family, supporting me in continuing my expressions. Especially my husband – I'm grateful for his honesty and willingness to aid in my dreams.

Bonnie, friend, I owe you much thanks for the inspiration of "The Hanging Tree." You painted the picture perfectly for a fantastic and morbid discussion.

I have a special place in my heart for Cammie, Mary, and Vanessa, my dearest writing friends. They are pillars to me, and I owe my writing growth to them. I appreciate their support – they are there for me in word and deed. Always.

I'm so excited and grateful to have my anthology with Monster Ivy. They've helped me to polish and shine each piece, and I'm so proud of what my little collection has become. Many thanks to Monster Ivy for adding their incredible efforts to mine.

Without readers, a book is pretty much just a stack of papers with a pretty cover. So, dear Reader, thank you for opening this book and flipping the pages. I sincerely appreciate every word you bring to life.

ABOUT THE AUTHOR

Katie Coughran is a multi-genre author of the Clean & Quirky Romance series, along with the Broden and Cookie chapter books. She has also published shorter works in anthologies, contributed to The Faithful Creative magazine, and recently published the first book in her non-fiction series, How to be a Minimalist With Kids: Finding Your Kind of Minimalism. When she isn't writing, you're likely to find Katie hanging out with her foxy husband and awesome kids in their motorhome in which they live full-time.

You can find out more and follow along at KatieCoughran.com or on Instagram. And, as ever, Katie would greatly appreciate it if you would post a review of *It Calls Me: An Anthology* anywhere online. Thank you!

ALSO BY KATIE COUGHRAN

The Clean & Quirky Romance Series – Romantic Comedies with all the feels

-- Happy Scoops

-- Twenty-Five Candles (available in paperback or free on KatieCoughran.com)

-- A Boyfriend for Graduation

The Broden and Cookie Series – Fans of the Magic Treehouse collection will enjoy these chapter books about a boy and his supernatural chicken

-- Broden and the Shark-Toothed Chicken

-- Broden and the Jellybean

-- Broden Wants to Quit

The Devils You Meet on Christmas Day:

A collection of dark and twisty Christmas stories

How to Be a Minimalist Series – Helping you define your minimalism and live an experience-rich life

-- How to Be a Minimalist With Kids: Finding Your Kind of Minimalism

DISCUSSION QUESTIONS

1. Some people are more affected by seasons than others. Some need sunshine; others prefer the rain. What about you? Do you know someone who struggles to "escape the gray" in a particular season?

2. Jealousy has a way of holding us back. What do you think Emmett in "The House that John Built" could have done to curb his jealousy when he was younger? Do you think it would have made a difference?

3. Coughran said she visited the exact location of "The Hanging Tree" and that you would never catch her out there at night. Do you think places, in and of themselves, can exude a positive or negative presence? If so, when have you experienced this?

4. "At the Crossroads" talks about two paths, but each has many different names. What are some of them? Do you think Coughran would say these paths choose us or we choose them?

5. Sometimes, a writer can paint us a picture while sparing us the unnecessary details. Jesse, for instance, in "The Ghost that Wore Rouge," took Maggie to a secret spot to get fresh with her, and we get the idea without seeing every single detail. Why do you think Coughran wrote it this way? How well do you think she pulled it off?

6. We all return to our childhood homes at some point. In "Coming Back," Coughran paints a rich tapestry of emotions. If you were to return home in five years from now, how would you feel? Which of your emotions do you think would mirror Coughran's?

THE DEVILS YOU MEET ON CHRISTMAS DAY: AN ANTHOLOGY

THE SKELETON KEY BY KATIE COUGHRAN

THE YOUNG MAN had been waiting at the table a long time. Or maybe it just seemed so due to the carefully wrapped package that rested in his coat pocket, nagging at him incessantly. Sitting alone, frequently checking his pocket watch, George was anxious for the arrival of Miss Trussell, in whom he had special interest.

George's mind wandered – as it often did – considering the necessary move to his new home that had been incredibly difficult. At the same time, it was one of the greatest blessings of his life. *If it weren't for Andrea Trussell, though, I would be miserable and completely out of my mind.*

Looking around, George happily observed the decorations in the main hall of the communal lodgings he called home. The Christmas tree in the corner was decorated with ornaments and brightly glowing candles, garlands were strung around, and there were wreaths on the doors that led to the kitchen and entryway. *It's rather difficult to tell that the paint is peeling and the wallpaper is coming off in this charming light,* George thought, trying to distract himself from checking his pocket watch once more.

I wonder what it would take to get that wallpaper changed out for something new and fashionable, he considered, still unused to his abode, which was much humbler than the estate he was supposed to have inherited. Sighing and looking at the table setting, George sat up straighter. *It doesn't matter, though, I suppose. As long as Mara is here, too –*

Catching the wrong name as it crossed his mind, George blushed a little, then shook his head. Correcting himself, he mumbled aloud, "I mean, as long as *Andrea* is here, too, I suppose nothing else matters."

Right at that moment, George's thoughts were cut off when Andrea came through the door, her attendant walking alongside, supporting her. Standing up, George's eyes widened, and a smile spread across his face. *It's no wonder I confuse her with Mara. She looks just like her – so lovely with her bright red lips and dark hair that I wish I could see let down. I'm sure it falls below her waist.*

Visions and memories of Mara came to mind, and they were so powerful, George felt as though he had traveled to another place and time. Especially when he thought of the first night he'd met Mara.

It had been cold out, but the ballroom was filled with laughter, friends, and dancing – enough to warm their souls and lift any spirits that had long been suffering. As soon as he took in the scene, the jovial dance music playing, candles lighting the room, exquisitely fine food and drink piled up on tables, George knew the night would be special.

Using his very best manners, George went directly to the host and hostess, ready to give thanks and compliments for the night of festivities. "Mr. and Mrs. Gardner, what a lovely evening. Thank you for including me. It's all wonderful, from your beautiful tree, to the lively music."

"Why, you are welcome, young Mr. Edwards," Mrs. Gardner said, smiling when he gave just a slight bow, indicating respect for both his and her rank. "We are glad to have you. Although, please tell your parents we are sorry they could not also attend."

"You are most gracious," George said, trying his best to smile, though he knew there was a hint of sadness to it. His mother had been unwell for some time, and it had taken a toll on his father. Always keeping to her rooms, George's father paid his mother the keenest attention, though George thought it might drive him mad someday. *One can only stay trapped in a room with such an unwell person for so long before it takes effect. Like some kind of emotional contagion.*

"I wish your mother well," Mrs. Gardner said kindly. Then, her tone brightening, she said, "Now, let us think of something else. You're a fine young man and came to dance; let's find a partner for you."

Taking a moment to look around the room, Mrs. Gardner's eyes widened when she saw a young woman whose back was turned to them. "I have just the young lady for you, Mr. Edwards – my niece. Come with me a moment."

Holding his arm out, George escorted Mrs. Gardner past the dancers. Cutting through several onlookers, they came to a young woman wearing a beautiful, deep blue satin gown, her dark, almost-black hair pulled up and decorated with little white flowers.

"Miss Voss," Mrs. Gardner said loudly, as only older women could do and still maintain socially acceptable manners. Excitement for the evening filling him, George was anxious to make introductions and join the others on the ballroom floor. "I have a young friend for you to meet and dance with."

Although George liked a pretty woman as much as the next man, at his somewhat young age of eighteen, he hadn't yet met one who inflicted total and instant infatuation on him. Until Miss Voss turned around.

As soon as she faced George, however, he could see the depths of her gray eyes, ruby red lips, and enticingly smooth skin. And the moment he felt the primal, gripping, demanding urge to draw close to, kiss, and touch Miss Voss' soft skin, George knew he was a changed man. And that he would never be the same.

"Miss Voss, this is Mr. George Edwards," Mrs. Gardner said, smiling knowingly as her niece looked shyly at the besotted Mr. Edwards.

"It is my great pleasure to meet you, Miss Voss," George said, and couldn't help himself when he took her gloved hand and kissed it.

"The pleasure is mine," she replied, her cheeks turning rosy.

"May I have the next dance?" George asked, his heart pounding as he wondered if she would accept his request.

With a slight nod of her head, Miss Voss agreed, saying, "Gladly."

The night was full of dancing, and mostly with Miss Voss. Along with the cheerful music, her bright yet shy expression and kind words kept him warm. And George experienced a new feeling; there was great discomfort in his core every time Mara was taken from him. It moved George so much that he couldn't tell whether it was pleasure or pain he felt as he anticipated their next rendezvous at the food table or on the ballroom floor.

Too soon, guests began departing, and George knew that etiquette required he take his leave as well.

"Miss Voss, it was my great pleasure to meet you tonight," he said, bowing and smiling warmly. "I do hope our paths will soon cross."

"As do I, Mr. Edwards," Mara replied, her complexion glowing.

Riding home in the carriage, George's mind wasn't tired, but awakened; it was alert and provoked by Mara. Before his mother had taken ill, Mrs. Edwards had often encouraged him to find a wife. A good, sweet woman who would make him happy. And, though he knew it was utterly ridiculous to choose a wife after an evening of dancing, George felt he couldn't help himself. He was smitten.

Though the Christmas ball had taken place just a year previous, the memories were as fresh to George as the moment when he had met Mara. They were so vivid that – had Andrea not appeared – George would have happily sat and recounted them in his mind. *I remember everything from the time spent with her family, to our picnic, and even that final, horrible night.*

"Miss Trussell," George said, fighting to focus on the woman in present company, not the ghosts of his past. Stepping forward, he gave Andrea his arm, relieving the attendant. Carefully, George helped Andrea to the table, steadying her when her troubled leg seemed to collapse a little as it was often wont to do.

"Hello, Mr. Edwards," Andrea replied, her voice as sweet as her eyes. "And how do you do this evening?"

"I am well ... now that you're here. And you?"

Blushing a little, Miss Trussell bowed her head slightly, saying, "I'm *very* well, Mr. Edwards."

Soon, the service brought out soup and – steam rising and bringing with it the herb-filled aroma, the delightful Christmas Eve supper had begun. Smiling at each other over their festive meal, they spoke of Christmases past, family they would miss seeing for the holiday, and joined in when spontaneous caroling was brought on by a group of boarders.

The singing had begun with a young man, not much older than George, who raised his glass and started up with, "Deck the Halls." The next moment, all at his table – most of whom were musicians who often jaunted around together – quickly picked up the tune. Still carrying their drinks, they walked up to the front of the room, singing so loudly, the great hall was filled with the beautiful sound.

Charlie, one of George's particular friends, disappeared no more than a moment, returning with an accordion he masterfully played. It was such a treat, and their music was so cheerful, it was impossible to resist joining in as they sang carol after carol.

Although he enjoyed the wonderful surprise, more than anything, George took great pleasure in watching Andrea's eyes shine brightly with happiness. *I forgot how much she loves to sing. I must make more opportunities for her to do so; I'm certain Charlie would comply any time I asked him to pull out his accordion.* To George, Andrea was delightful, with her voice that joined in like a songbird, her delicate hands that clapped in time, and her laugh that sounded like the tinkling of bells.

When supper was eaten, accompanied by the enchanting music, George became much more aware of the package in his pocket than he had been all night. One of the young women began singing "Silent Night" with the loveliest voice he'd ever heard, and George's heart was so full, he knew he *had* to take courage and offer the package to Andrea. *It'll be all right, good fellow. It won't be the same as with Mara; Andrea is different and ... we're here.* Without *meddling aunts.*

With the sounds of the accordion and song mingling together, George stood and quietly dropped down on one knee. Looking at Andrea, he *knew* it was the right thing – and that he couldn't wait another moment to speak. Eyes glittering with tears, Andrea put fingers to her lips, covering her lovely, red-lipped smile.

"Miss Trussell," George began, swallowing hard as he realized his heart was pounding quite a bit harder than it had been only moments prior. "You have turned my life from night to day. I was completely miserable – a *wretch* – before meeting you. And now I see that coming here has been a blessing ... because you're here."

"Oh, Mr. Edwards," Andrea said, becoming emotional. Face beaming warmly as a teardrop moved down her cheek, George felt encouraged to continue onward.

"I hope I have made you just as happy. And if not, I would spend my lifetime trying," George said in a whisper just louder than the sweet music. "Please ... *please* bless me the rest of my days by agreeing to be my wife."

Pulling the package out of his breast coat pocket, George meekly held it out to Andrea, whose cheeks were rosier than ever. With the enchanting music weaving its way through the room, the candlelight seeming to dance in time to its quiet beat, George couldn't think of a more perfect time to ask Andrea to be his wife. *Perhaps the magic of the night can will her to say yes.*

Just as Andrea's delicate fingers took the package from

his hands, however, the spell was broken. Though he hadn't noticed, the music stopped, and every guest in the hall was staring at them. From the front of the room where he'd been singing and playing his accordion, Charlie called, "Say *yes,* Miss Trussell!"

There was silence for a few seconds, which was abruptly disturbed by the housekeeper and a few of her staff. Watching as they rushed over, George looked at them quizzically, frustrated that they were disturbing the moment of utmost importance.

"Mr. Edwards," Mrs. Overton, the housekeeper, said, tone stern. "Your rooms are prepared for the evening, sir."

"Thank you, Mrs. Overton," George said, matching his attitude to hers. "I will retire shortly."

Nodding curtly at her, trying not to seem awkward from where he rested on his knee, George thought Mrs. Overton would go away. However, the attendants were looking at Mrs. Overton for instruction, and George began to fear the worst; he would not be given an opportunity to hear the answer to his proposal.

Rage suddenly overcame him as George looked at Mrs. Overton and the two men behind her. The image of her face changed in his mind, and it seemed as if Mrs. Gardner, Mara's aunt, were standing before him. Though he tried, George couldn't help the way his fist clenched, contrasting the meekness with which he had offered his gift to Andrea.

Vivid memories of his proposal to Mara assaulted him, making his face turn white as his mind strained, attempting to gain control. *God help me!*

George remembered everything, from the pure white dress Mara was wearing, to the angrily-shouted words of Mrs. Gardner when Mara's red lips whispered the glorious acceptance George had hoped to hear. Though he'd never meant to lose his temper as he was wont to do, images came to George's mind of his maniacal reaction to Mrs. Gardner's foul-mouthed objection and threats, both verbal and physical.

And he remembered Mara stepping between them as the occurrence escalated, George losing his sanity completely. Although his face remained as hard and cold as a stone while looking up at Mrs. Overton, George cringed at the ghostly memory that came next. The moment when the same red of Mara's lips appeared on her cheek when George accidentally struck Mara instead of her wretched aunt. Wincing at the vision, George felt the same despair he'd experienced upon seeing her flesh swollen and broken open, bright red blood spilling from the wound.

Eyes shifting down to his fist, George slowly rose to his feet, towering above Mrs. Overton as he had Mrs. Gardner. *I swore it would never happen again; not just because I was forced to come to this god-awful prison of the insane.*

Looking around at the room and its inhabitants with wide-open eyes, George silently admitted that he often lied to himself; it was the only way to survive. Feeling short of breath from his suddenly clear vision, the awareness of his tendency to imagine his life differently struck George, and he saw the attendants as wardens, the occupants as mental patients.

Surveying the room as the music began once again, instead of hearing finely trained musicians, his ears were assaulted as half of the voices in the ragtag choir began making awful sounds he'd thought could only come from a cat. And out of his peripheral vision, George caught sight of two men who reminded him of the true reason the wall-paper needed to be replaced.

Turning his head to watch them, he once again felt

deep compassion. Unattended, they clawed at the wall, the winter making their lives feel that much more entombed and unbearable. Clenching his jaw, George knew many of his fellow guests took to picking at the wallpaper because the stifling winter and lack of outdoor occupation drove them even *more* mad. It didn't seem to matter how often their hands were slapped, they continued picking as a prisoner in a hold might scratch at the walls. A desperate and vain struggle to achieve freedom.

Although the candlelight seemed bright to him, George acknowledged that it was only so because a few extra candles were granted as a Christmas gift, adding to the meager light of their daily existence. It was for the same reason that their supper seemed so festive. The muck that was usually thrown down before them had been made with ingredients a few days fresher and was composed of two dishes instead of one.

But Andrea, he hadn't imagined. Allowing his eyes to rest on her, George could see that. The lovely sight of her made his hand relax, and George knew that Andrea was every bit as wonderful as he believed her to be. He *knew* she was so, even without his imagination that worked to exhaustion in an effort to turn the horror of a house into a barely livable habitat.

"This way, Mr. Edwards," Mrs. Overton said once more, then turned to Andrea's attendant that had appeared, nodding at the woman he loved. "And *your* rooms are ready as well, Miss Trussell."

Choosing to remain silent as Andrea slowly walked away, leaning the weight of her slight body on her attendant's arm, George struggled to keep hold of his control. Considering what he would say and do, George slowly turned his eyes to Mrs. Overton and the large men behind her.

"Mr. Edwards, you *do* remember *where* you are and those actions which brought you here?" Mrs. Overton hissed. And – though Mrs. Overton clearly believed George had forgotten – he knew *too* well where he was. And as to the *why*, George clearly recalled his disgraceful actions, Mara's malicious aunt who had forced a trial, and his less-than-capable advocates of parents.

"I remember, Mrs. Overton," George replied, his jaw clenched so tightly the words could barely slip through his teeth.

"Well, then, you will understand why there won't be proposals or marriage, Mr. Edwards," Mrs. Overton said, her voice like iron.

There was silence between them, making all who were even slightly mentally aware completely uncomfortable. Anger welled up, and George thought he might explode.

But right when his fist began to clench again, an image of Andrea – not Mara – slowly came to his mind. Although he hated Mrs. Overton and the *supposedly* humane asylum where the unseemly of the wealthy were hidden away, George knew that a life with Andrea would be impossible if he acted on his emotions.

"Goodnight, Mrs. Overton," he said. With one tug at the bottom of his coat, George straightened his attire, then stiffly walked to his dark, cold room, closing the door behind him. Only lit by a single candle, George was glad he couldn't see the ragged comforter that barely kept him warm, the tattered couch he didn't like to sit on, or the wash stand with its cracked basin. They only added to the reality he tried to hide from.

Returning to pretending, George ignored the fact that a

key was inserted into the lock from the outside, trapping him in for the night. It was easy to do; much more difficult was the task of forgetting the pain he felt at not knowing whether Andrea would have him. Or how.

In the middle of the night, a slight, shadowy figure silently made her way down the hall, a dark robe over her dressing gown. Long, dark hair fell below her waist and, had there been enough light, one would be able to see her rosy cheeks and red lips.

Although she let on that it was difficult to move without assistance, it wasn't the truth. *Not even George knows, though I'll soon tell him.* At some point within the time of her appalling imprisonment, Andrea's injuries from the failed attempt at a suicidal fall had healed. The gained mobility had come on slowly, and as soon as she suspected it, Andrea knew it must remain a secret.

Shuddering, Andrea slipped into a little nook when she heard movement ahead. Waiting for them to walk on, she thought, *Let alone being punished for hiding the truth, I couldn't tolerate them locking my door at night or treating me like everyone else ...*

When all was quiet once more, Andrea soon found George's door. Silently inserting the skeleton key into the lock, she prayed the door wouldn't creak when she pushed it open. Letting herself in and closing the thankfully quiet door behind her, Andrea slowly walked toward the bed where George was peacefully sleeping.

Moving forward with a soft smile spreading across her lips, Andrea eyed George with his smooth skin, masculine body, and lips she *ached* to feel on hers. Considering how genteel the thought *wasn't,* Andrea cocked her eyebrow and moved closer; *I don't care if it's ladylike or not. I'm not a true lady anymore, anyway – am I?*

Just close enough to hear the soft breath come in and out of George's slightly open mouth, Andrea reached out, gently running her hand through his tousled, dark hair. Sighing, she smiled, letting her fingers feel his soft lengths once more.

"George," Andrea whispered, touching his cheek. A drowsy groan slipped through his lips and, trying to wake him, Andrea moved her hand along his striking jawline, neck, shoulder. "George – I'm here. Wake up."

Drowsily coming to, George slowly opened his eyes. Without questioning how she was there, George took her hand, kissed it, then held it to his chest as he closed his eyes once more.

"George, no. Don't go back to sleep," Andrea said, a delighted, suppressed laugh escaping her lips. "George, please. I've come with your package."

Perhaps it was her persistence, or mention of the package, but George finally woke up, his eyes shocked and clearly aware. "Miss Trussell? What – how – what's happening?"

"Call me Andrea," she said, smiling warmly. "I'm here because, well, I was never able to open your gift."

"But, how did you get here? You must feel *very* unwell –" George began when Andrea cut him off.

"George, I managed without trouble, and we'll talk about that later," Andrea said softly, pulling her hand free and moving it through his hair once more, making his eyes close for the slightest moment as he let out a deep sigh. "It's Christmas now, George. Shall I open my present?"

"One moment, please," George said, the tightness of his voice gone. Sitting up and kindly taking the package from her, George got out of bed, pulling his robe on, and leading Andrea to the somewhat ragged sofa.

Falling to one knee for the second time that night, George took Andrea's hand. Lightly kissing it, he spoke in a whisper that sent a tickle down her back. "Andrea, will you be my wife – no matter what they say or where we are?"

Without hesitation, her face bright, Andrea quickly responded with a joyful, *"Yes."*

Holding the package out, Andrea took it, carefully pulling on one end of the string, then unfolding the paper. There, sitting in the middle of the wrapping, was a thin band of gold. George took it, the brown paper falling to the floor as he did so. Holding her hand, George slipped the ring onto her finger, Andrea smiling as he did so.

Then, leaning forward, George's arms were wrapping around Andrea, drawing her as close as possible. Entwining her arms around George in return, Andrea took a deep breath, taking in his manly scent and glorious warmth – something Andrea never thought she would be able to do. And, even though she knew the ring on her finger and man in her arms had once been Mara's, they were *hers* now.

Raising his head, George stood and powerfully yet gently pulled Andrea to her feet. And then, the lips she so admired were kissing hers. Softly, they caressed hers, moving slowly, as if he were savoring her mouth, making Andrea feel completely out of breath.

George gently pressed his lips against hers once more, then, as with great difficulty, pulled away. "You must return to your room, Andrea. No one can know."

"And no one shall," she whispered, gently stroking his arm before walking away.

Standing in the doorway, she turned around and looked at George once more, waving her pale hand. Slipping out,

Andrea closed the door behind her. As she did so, locking him in once more, the twitch of a smile danced on her lips. And, although her feelings for George were sincere, she couldn't help but find it delightful to turn the key.

Just as she did every night.

To read the full collection of macabre stories, purchase the ebook, audiobook, or paperback at your favorite retailer online! If you liked The Riverwalk, another Soulmate Seekers story can be found in this anthology, too.

www.ingramcontent.com/pod-product-compliance
Lightning Source LLC
Chambersburg PA
CBHW070448170726
48291CB00005B/1657

9781948095228